ZAFTIG
WELL ROUNDED EROTICA

ZAFTIG

WELL ROUNDED EROTICA

Edited by

Hanne Blank

Published in the United States by Cleis Press Inc.,

P.O. Box 14684, San Francisco, California 94114.

Printed in the United States.

Cover design: Scott Idleman

Text design: Karen Quigg

Logo art: Juana Alicia

First Edition.

10 9 8 7 6 5 4 3 2 1

LIBRARY OF CONGRESS CATALOGING-IN-PUBLICATION DATA

Zaftig : well rounded erotica / edited by Hanne Blank.— 1st ed.

       p. cm.

     ISBN 1-57344-122-8 (pbk. : alk. paper)

      1. Erotic stories, American. 2. Overweight persons—Fiction. I. Blank, Hanne.

PS648.E7 Z34 2001

813'.01083538—dc21   00-065633

CONTENTS

INTRODUCTION

Hanne Blank

Zaftig, in Yiddish, means *juicy.* It also means voluptuous, plump, and round in a deliciously sensuous sort of way. Used to refer to people's bodies, it suggests opulence and abundance, a sort of unconventional beauty built on heft and curves and softness. *Zaftig* is also, often, a euphemism for saying that someone is fat.

This is why I find the word so charming, and use it so frequently, not least as the title for this book. Fat people—no question about it—are not normally thought of in this culture as being juicy and voluptuous, sensuous and delicious. Our bodies aren't usually characterized as opulent or beautiful, the weight and solidity of our curves not commonly praised, at least in public. In this day and age, thin has never been more in, and it seems like a peek into some alien dimension to look back at magazine ads from the 1940s and early 1950s—like one I have pinned to the wall of my office—that reassuringly promise weight gain and "exciting curves" to skinny girls.

But the truth of the matter is that whether bigger bodies are currently in vogue, and whether the culture we live in appreciates the many glories of bodies of diverse types and sizes, the sensual appeal of the generous, well-upholstered body, with all its curves and full, firm swells of flesh, has never really gone out of style. Whether merely pleasingly plump or flat-out fat, women and men whose bodies are bigger and heavier than the so-called "norm" have always had their following, and they continue to be the objects of lustful and affectionate attention even in these Slim-Fast times.

It is a great honor for me, as well as an enormous personal pleasure, to present this collection of erotic stories in celebration of those big bodies, those round bodies, those chubby-plump-voluptuous-heavy fat bodies of all sizes of large. Within these pages you will find the words and voices of a wide variety of women of a great many shapes and sizes, both established writers and first-timers, writing about size, sex, and sultry satisfaction from a panoply of perspectives that prove that only our imaginations—not body size or weight—can possibly limit the possibilities of our sexuality.

The characters who populate these pages are as diverse, as normal, and as intriguing as fat people are themselves. They are lesbian, gay, straight, and bi; kinky and vanilla; coupled and single. They have sex in dressing rooms, in dorms, at BDSM clubs, in parking lots and bathtubs, and even in their bedrooms, just like you and me. Also just like you and me, the characters in this book are extremely emotionally real, running the gamut from silly to somber, delighted to distraught, offering us visceral, affecting glimpses into the spirit and soul of being sexual in and with bodies that do not conform to the ideal.

As a result, although this book is definitely sexual, sensual, and arousing, it is also challenging—not always an easy or comfortable book to read. Sexuality, for people who don't conform to what our culture depicts as ideal, can seem inextricably entwined with fear, shame, and worry. Some of the stories in this book explore that damage, like Eleanor Brown's elegant and insightful "Breathing Lessons." However, as Brown's ultimately triumphant narrative so sweetly concludes, this psychological adversity breeds a glorious strength and a resilient, brave, often heart-stoppingly intense sexuality.

Through this intense sexuality, and through the intense ways that the sexuality in this book is rooted in the complex and constantly changing personal and political relationship that exists between us, our bodies, and our culture, we get a glimpse not only of ways in which these stories are the stories of every one of us who has ever had a moment's worry or fear about the worth of our bodies, but also of the timeless, ineffable grace of love and lust. Whether done with irreverent, bold humor, as in Ann Tourney's "How Loretta Got a Schlong"; vivid imagination, as in Melusine's "Looking, Really Looking at a Painting"; or simply through evocative, beautiful storytelling, as in Jianda Johnson's "Divining," Corbie Petulengro's "In Season," and many others—these stories open up portholes not only into the lives of their characters, but also into our own.

These are stories that recognize the liberatory power of sex. Many of the pieces in this book are very frank in celebrating the transformative force of sex, lust, desire, and the recognition that one is desired, engendering a joyful and sexy undercurrent of rebelliousness throughout the book, an easy, soft smile that hints at the rewards of shucking conventional cultural norms in favor of the things that truly fulfill.

To read this book and to let yourself be emotionally and sexually carried away by its stories is to join a tender and subversive conspiracy: As we read stories like Catherine Lundoff's "The Model," Heather Corinna's "Mädchen in Uniform," and Debra Hyde's "Flesh Love," there can be no denying that these people, these bodies that are so far from what our culture's images want us to think of as ideally sexually attractive, are utterly worthy of our admiration, our adoration, our unapologetic dirt-pawing do-me-now lust. Certainly there are enough different flavors and styles of that lust here, from Saachi Green's soulful "Etched in the Flesh" to Veronica Kelly's intimate "Weekdays at Rosini's Bakery" to Lori Selke's zesty "Big Girls, Little Girls," to thoroughly prime the imagination.

This is volatile smut. It is succulent and dangerous, excessive and vulnerable. The words and ideas contained in this book will push your buttons, will make you think, will make you wonder about yourself and your attitudes about sex and bodies. The images and scenarios will, I hope, make your nerves sizzle and your panties wet (yes, even if you're a boy) with yearning. Most of all, it will make you look at your own body, and the bodies of the people around you, with a wider view toward what might move and inspire you to lust and love and lusciousness.

I extend my deep gratitude to all of the contributors to this book, and to the many people whose encouragement and friendship continue to help make my work a reality: Liz Tamny, Lynn McAfee, Janet Hardy, Gil Rodman, Kim Airs, M. Christian, Claire Cavanah, Frédérique Delacoste, Felice Newman, and Heather Corinna. Thanks also to Raven Kaldera for being a breath of fresh air, Simon Sheppard for the inspiration, Jack Dietz for grace in heavy traffic, Rhetta Wiley and Thomas K.

Lewis for the gold lamé, and Deb Malkin for being succulent, dangerous, and beautiful. Most of all, my thanks, my devotion, and my love go to my beloved life partner, Malcolm Gin, to whom I dedicate this book.

Hanne Blank
Jamaica Plain, Massachusetts
January 2001

LOOKING, REALLY LOOKING AT A PAINTING

Melusine

1. Observation

I pause, standing in the gallery, my boots thunk-squeaking their rubber soles across the floor. The guard in the corner moves on to the next room, leaving me in silence, looking, admiring, lusting.

As befits any fine courtesan, she is painted as Venus, although she started as an actress, smearing on greasepaint rather than preening with doves. She looks out at me, a forward, come-hither, come-hotter glance, brown curls cascading over her shoulders, sloe eyes shimmering and her body lush, exquisite. She is in copper silk, gleaming, clinging tightly to her flesh, luxuriant, her waist cinched with a corset, showing her full, curvy hips, breasts swelling out from the busk—one bare, the other barely covered with a wrap of the silk, letting the curves peek through. And her jewels! She has ropes of pearls, wound in her hair, draped around her neck, twining along her skin, like a come-splashed tribute to her fleshy splendor. An old joke, but oh god she wears it well. There is so much to touch, so much to taste, and the painted blushes at her throat make me hunger. Seeing the valley between her breasts, I think about burying my face between them, tonguing along the soft skin heavy with sweat, musk, the heat of the unending, painted-summer afternoon.

I am suddenly, shamelessly wet at the thought of this, of tonguing the nipples that a merry monarch compared to rubies, corals, flames of love alight; I think of the apocryphal tales of his sport in bed with his favorites, her and two others at once. Perhaps they are the two in the background dressed as allegorical figures Grace and Temperance (O painterly irony!), draped in gauze with strings of emeralds and rubies wrapped around their throats, hair sausage-curled in red and gold ringlets, hips ample under the sheer gauze, hint of round, soft bellies and delicious breasts hanging heavy like ripe fruit. Three Goddesses, Three Graces, I think—and think of how many men had spent themselves thinking of the ladies sporting in the royal bedchamber, how many art historians had surreptitiously retired to the men's room to squirt themselves into an ironed handkerchief, thinking about their faces buried between musky thighs, imagined rubbing themselves to hardness against the milky spheres of the slut Venus's grabbable, fuckable ass, oh jeezus, and I think of the kind of picture we would paint together, the Three Graces and I.

II. Banquet

Her flesh is white and reddens like cherries and cream when I bite, sinking my teeth into her shoulder, soothing it with my tongue, taking one breast in my hand, overflowing, heavy, more than a handful is beyond, so far beyond all right, rolling the pink nipple between my thumb and forefinger until she moans, rolling up her skirt to show white stockings gartered at the knee, heavy, white, solid sweet thighs, and the finest cunt in Christendom, all coral fringes and wet silk under the full swell of belly and coarse, dark curls. I feel her body quiver and shake as she slides her fingers in, frigging herself as I lick the back of her neck, biting and biting, grinding my own wet cunt against her, an unrepentant tribadist.

I am licking further and further down, along the roundness of her breasts, the lace marks left from the corset crossing flesh too much to stay contained, and I tongue furiously, wetting her skin, my face, diving to lick at the juncture of her thighs, burying my face in her dark curls, head clasped between her legs, the taste of flesh and salt, lapping at her fingers as she fucks herself again and again, screaming and moaning, seeing her body shake and quiver, feeling the flesh on her belly ripple with every move, every shuddering sigh.

She tastes of salt and musk and honey, and I could drink her dry, moving in long full strokes, covering my face with her fluids. Above me, her cries are drowned in kisses; Temperance is kissing, golden hair grown curled and wet from exertion, grinding and grinding, and as I lick I feel Grace's breasts at my back, nipples growing hot and hard as my cunt drips. I am drunk on flesh and the taste of women known for pleasure; but now no men spend, now the finest courtesans play alone, away from prying eyes, and I am richer than any wastrel king. My tongue is entrenched in Venus's cunt. Closing my eyes, I lick and lick as if my life depended on it, working her clit with my tongue and teeth, flicking the rosy flesh until her legs scissor around my head and my face is bathed with moisture, filling my mouth, my nostrils, till all I taste and breathe is her, her now-sticky fingers twined in my hair.

It is then, with my eyes closed, face dripping, that I feel hands on my breasts, squeezing, pinching, Temperance's light fingers running over the full swelling of my belly to reach my cunt, pinching it again and again between her fingers, as I moan my pleasure back into the mass of flesh before me. Venus's legs are wider, and I am licking from clit to cunt to asshole, sliding and slipping back and forth, lips vibrating as Temperance tweaks my clit, electrifying me.

It is then that I feel cruel Grace, hear her chuckle behind me, feel a pair of hands spread me open, sense a wet, slippery tongue licking around my asshole, making me scream into the wet, fleshy thighs, buck against Temperance's heavy arms and breasts in pleasure, and sob as, one by one, I am violated, pearl by pearl, by the necklace that Grace is sliding into my asshole, wiggling it back and forth. Then I am full and all is tongues and flesh and lips around me. I lick earlobes and wrists, toes and cunt, with fervor, enthusiasm, worshiping at the altar of graces and harlots, licking the rich curves of bellies and breasts, the sweet *S* of back and ass, drunk on flesh, on softness beneath and above me twisting and twisting. I hump thighs, calves, arms, still full of the necklace, feeling my head pushed back to Venus's gates, the king's favorite grotto, my shrine of lust, my site of hungry worship. And it is with my face buried in her cunt, her fingers scraping the back of my neck, Temperance's hungry fingers at my clit, and Grace tugging the pearls from my ass that I come, a deep shudder, screaming into the flesh of harlots, dripping fluids growling, screaming smothered by breasts and hips and hot white thighs, the electricity building and building until I burst and burst at another caress, a final hip twitch, the last squeeze of my asshole as it releases the last two pearls....

I squeeze my thighs together, discreetly still admiring the painting. The guard passes through, ambling slowly in blue, and I exit, breath still heavy, cunt still slick, still sweetly drunk on flesh.

DIVINING

Jianda Johnson

Zane and I christen my living room with our bodies. We bump walls. I scream when I come. And again. My bed creaks to the breaking point. Neighbors pitch fits. They bump walls back. Fuck them, I'm fucking.

We bless my new apartment with our sweat and breath, rising like Nagchampa, falling like glitter. My kitchen counter is our altar. Underneath air vents that blow cool air above us, it's me, bent over. It's Zane and his right hand flowing back and forth underneath my bum. Then his left. The pressure of the pads of his palms asserts itself hard, then arduously harder. A finger finds my panties—success—jiggles with the lock hidden inside my lips until it loosens, wet.

Zane's own hard finds and feels for me but does not knock. Just his index finger, then a pinkie, taking turns motioning "come here" inside me at speeds gone delirious.

Over now, spent, we lie in the kitchen, giggling like kindergartners with our own secret stories.

• • •

This is joy inside my tears. Salesgirl lets this man I barely know into the dressing room at Lane Bryant. I gasp.

("You're together, right? You're together?" Salesgirl blushes.) I nod.

Zane closes the door behind us. I try on peach, frilly underthings he's hand-picked. Then, a burgundy bra. Then amber. Black.

("That one," he says, "and that." Zane chooses peach delicacies, and burgundy, this time. There are and always will be other times.)

Smiling, ceremonious, I sashay up to the cash register. These fabrics made of silk, of velvet, they are Queen and Goddesswear, bras for a dear little girl who never knew she had the right to fuck—not even someday.

• • •

This is us in my narrow, short hallway. Zane unfurls a dark brown towel and lays it before me.

("Not quite a red carpet, but it'll do," he volunteers.) I think he's kidding. He stares, unflinching.

Hallway lovemaking. I stare up at the crystal chandelier I inherited from an angry, bony grandma. This is all she gave me. Here now, Zane gives me head. I reclaim the old heirloom. My body shivers as revelations overlap one another, resolving in my body.

All things good and wonderful flow forth from my pussy. My vagina hums; I sing in harmony alongside her, lulled into a satisfied sleep on my own carpet. Safe.

Zane kneads underneath my bottom like a cat, drawing from the well of a mother's nectar. Or, like a boy. Like a wide-eyed human animal at play, fascinated.

Heartening. Soul of my soul. This is my first waking thought as he's perched up on one arm, welcoming me back to the world.

"Morning," says he.

• • •

Zane. This is you, your small, pink tongue tracing shapes along my belly (my most sensitive, most injured part, the onus of activity since the day of my birth). You whoosh sounds into my ears like "Mmm" and "Aaahh," and I feel gorgeous. I *am*. I am your natural papaya. Exotic and abundant drinking gourd, overflowing.

Ecstatic, a howl overtakes me as your mouth revivifies my pussy. I cannot cry. I moan from a dark center, my honey boils. You taste it. Your face is a boy's face, his darling neck craned up toward imaginary countertops, sucking out the sweetness from the center of dessert and begging, "More please?"

You like my candy. It softens your bitter. Makes us even.

"God," I coo, "good." My legs part open, you slide your hands, gingerly up and over, your fingers hover just above my heat, twirling in small circles. You're divining for my sweet. And she does come.

• • •

This is autoerotic. Some days later… I barely get a chance to turn off the shower, nozzle pointing at my mound. Your glance follows along my neck to my cocoa-honey nipples. Then breasts. I open myself to you, my heart beating in between. Full, round tits spill into your hands. Your palms face up in innocent supplication.

You, devotee, worshipping my curves and folds, your hands face the heaven of my softness, reverent, the way things should be.

My mind thinks back to warm, cozy childhood baths. Doting parents gush forth words like "baby fat" and "adorable" in cool, dulcet love-tones. When and why the doting stopped had everything to do with my size. For years, I hated that.

Your tongue carries on the dance, oblivious, hopeful, traveling toward its destination, relentless, feeling its way to my fountain.

You pause, torn. You reach toward my face to stroke it. (No Zane, that's after. Stay low and push lower. Harder.) You obey, continue. You hum softly, quiet even in your loving. I overcompensate: A Big Momma scream evinces herself.

You are taller than me. Wider. My first big man. I used to make love to stickmen, did you know that? Does it matter? You are tender in your touching. That's what matters.

• • •

My desire, latent no more, is fluid, aqua. Starving.

Along comes Zane, to satiate her:

Cock submerged between my fat thighs of silk, seeks its way to my pussy of velvet. Rams, repeats, relents, and again, on and on, this day, that, and the day after that, and on Christmas and my Pop's birthday, even on All Saints Day.

This is my head nestled in the cradle of his lap, old Hardy rouses from a curled-up sleep, raises his chubby head, and lets me suck.

This is taking the pseudo butch in her own bed and softening her. Rubbing her clit like a shiny new jewel with no second thoughts or hesitation, no "lose weight" this or "diet" that.

This is us, taking our sweet time.

HOW LORETTA GOT A SCHLONG

Anne Tourney

Later she would wonder if that afternoon had been a fantasy, the orgy of a starved imagination. In client meetings or at the hairdresser's, Loretta would sometimes burst out laughing at the memory of her first blowjob. Not the first blowjob she had ever given—the first one she had gotten.

Could it really have happened? Loretta was a professional woman, a designer of high-tech kitchens where geometry and stainless steel prevailed over the primal comfort of food. She had always been emotionally stable, socially impeccable. Until last spring, she could never have imagined herself sporting her own meaty, mighty schlong. But she had a piece of evidence—well hidden, of course—that she had once possessed such a thing. The chewed end of Loretta's faux cock lay wrapped in cellophane at the back of her refrigerator. Sometimes, when she was contemplating the contents of her fridge, she caught a whiff of spiced meat, and that afternoon came back to her.

• • •

In March Loretta had planned to go to Acapulco with her best friend, Tamara, who was celebrating the final rupture with her almost-fiancé. The trip was supposed to be a raunchy escapade, a south-of-the-border adventure featuring tamer, much curvier versions of Thelma and Louise. When Tamara didn't show up at the airport an hour before the flight, Loretta felt a flutter of panic. But as the first passengers began to board the plane, the flutter escalated into a flapping hysteria. Two minutes before the final boarding call, Loretta's cell phone trilled. Tamara sobbed apologies. She was getting back together with Brad. He had finally produced a ring—with a diamond the size of an extracted wisdom tooth.

"What's the catch?" Loretta asked. "Let me guess. The ring is two sizes too small. All you have to do is lose forty pounds and you get to wear it."

Tamara gave a startled sniffle. "How did you know?"

"Because every woman he's slept with behind your back has been a size 6, Tam. Remember?"

Loretta left the airport and drove home through the foul gray afternoon. Safely back in her house, she stripped off her "Viva Acapulco" dress and put on the pink flannel granny gown that had hidden her flesh for more nights than she could count. She scrubbed the makeup off her face and tied up her thick curls with a wide elastic band. Then Loretta belly-flopped onto her bed, where she spent the rest of her vacation.

The week passed slowly. Loretta ordered a total of five pizzas, read three trashy novels, and watched thirty hours of television. In the midst of this swamp of overindulgence, she reflected on her life and realized that she was starving—in both body and soul. She had spent so much of her adult life designing kitchens where other people could perform the rituals of cooking, eating, sharing news and secrets, that she hadn't had time for any intimate rites of her own. In the past ten years she hadn't done much but work, bolt down solitary meals, and pay her bills.

Pay her bills?

Loretta fumbled for the clock on her nightstand. It was two forty-five on Friday afternoon. She had spent an entire week with no schedule, no plans. Loretta always planned everything. But last week, in her excitement over Mexico, she had forgotten to pay her Visa bill. If she didn't put it in the mail today, the bill would be late. Her interest rate would skyrocket. Some polite credit thug would call and threaten her with ruin. The last pickup of the day at her local post office was three o'clock. Loretta had fifteen minutes to save herself from financial humiliation.

She leaped out of bed so fast that her head spun. As she reached for her car keys on the dresser, she stumbled and fell. Lying in a heap on her bedroom floor, she looked up and caught the glitter of a yellow plastic raincoat hanging in her closet.

Fourteen minutes.

Loretta scrambled to her feet. She snatched the raincoat off its hanger and pulled it on over her nightie. Then she raced out the door and jumped into her car. As her foot reached for the gas pedal, her legs got tangled in the ankle-length skirt of her nightgown. Loretta bucked up and down in the seat until she had worked the gown above her waist. She grabbed the handfuls of fabric and twisted them into a long clump. Resourceful even in distress, Loretta pulled the elastic band from her hair and used it to secure the cloth between her thighs. With the wad of flannel bobbing at half-mast between her legs like a rosy appendage, Loretta backed the car out of her driveway.

Somehow, while she was lying in her darkened bedroom, the outdoor world had exploded. Ornamental cherry trees had erupted into bloom. Daffodils blared in every border garden on Loretta's street. The soil, dense from winter rains, had broken forth to release all kinds of dainty white-and-green things. Spring had come. Loretta eased her foot off the gas pedal and snuggled back against the driver's seat. Sunlight spangled her hands. Her yellow raincoat sparkled. Stopping at a traffic light, she looked around and smiled. Metamorphosis was everywhere. Who cared about a credit rating?

A Pacific Bell bucket truck pulled up beside her. The man high up in the passenger's seat glanced down at Loretta. He grinned and slid his thick, tanned forearm over the edge of the open window. The arm looked as succulent as roasted chicken. Loretta wanted to bite it, just to see if hot grease would spurt out.

"Nice schlong you got there, lady," the man said.

That's when the dream part began.

Loretta was flustered at first. Schlong? What was that? Some kind of primitive wind instrument? A slow burn crept up her neck as she remembered. *Schlong* was just another entry in that eternal work-in-progress, the Dictionary of Penile Slang.

The man's smile warmed and widened. He had white, slightly crooked teeth. Full, sun-chapped lips. Sky-high cheekbones. Sheaves of wheaty hair that might be blond, or gray. Along the curves of his arm, brown moles were scattered like flecks of chocolate. Flecks of chocolate melting in the sunlight, warm and waiting for Loretta's tongue. Loretta had a sudden vision of him fucking her against a telephone pole, her bare bottom harvesting splinters as he pushed her against the wood. Her pussy twitched. A starburst of pleasure warmed her loins.

Loretta glanced down at her lap, expecting to see a spreading stain of liquid arousal.

What she saw was a schlong. No doubt about it. The twisted mass of Loretta's pink nightgown rose between her thighs like a semi-erect penis. If the fluffy lump of flannel were a real phallus, it would be an impressive specimen. A prize-winning pecker. A schlong worthy of a superhero.

The traffic light changed. The truck lurched forward. Loretta's blue-collar fantasy looked back and waved. Loretta reached down to touch her new organ. It felt as harmless as a stuffed bunny, but it looked like a rod of reckoning. If only it could stand tall! If Loretta's schlong had the firm meatiness that characterizes every healthy hard-on, then the softness of the flannel would seem natural. Erections were supposed to be velvety to the touch. Even a little fuzziness wasn't out of place. All she needed was some substance under the skin.

A car horn beeped. Loretta drove through the intersection and headed in the opposite direction of the post office. The trajectory of her day had changed.

When she pulled into the supermarket parking lot, Loretta stopped to check her reflection in the rear-view mirror. Her eyes gleamed and her round cheeks were flushed, as if she had been gazing into an open oven in which some fragrant cake was baking. No lipstick today—her mouth was puffy, pale, and ripe. Her auburn curls, having been confined in a topknot for a week, rioted over her shoulders. In her yellow raincoat and pink nightie, she looked like a lunatic. A *gorgeous* lunatic.

Loretta picked up her purse, in which her Visa bill lay forgotten, and climbed out of the car. She tucked her schlong into her raincoat and buttoned the coat over her nightie. Strolling across the parking lot, she tried to look like an ordinary woman. It was perfectly natural to wear a raincoat at this time of year. A

few people cast curious looks at her crocheted slippers, but
Loretta ignored them. Underneath her coat, an extraordinary
secret hummed.

As she walked up to the supermarket deli, Loretta slid her
hand into her pocket and touched the schlong. A reedy woman
with a cap of frosted hair walked by, pushing a shopping cart.
She looked at Loretta, almost acknowledged her, and then
averted her eyes. The woman's name was Sandra Thwaite-
Barnside. Loretta had designed her kitchen. Sandra had
challenged Loretta's opinion on cabinet handles, and the women
had gotten into one of those chilly, feline standoffs that Loretta
always lost. Loretta had ended up giving Sandra the zinc grips
she wanted, though the kitchen cried out for the homey touch of
porcelain knobs. In spite of that capitulation, the woman had
never sent the last installment of Loretta's fee. Loretta would
have pursued the debt, but she didn't have the guts.

Or the schlong.

"Hi, there," Loretta said brightly. "You're Sandra Thwaite-
Barnside, aren't you? I worked on your kitchen last year. You
know what? I never got your final payment."

The woman raised her eyebrows. "My kitchen? What payment? I don't think I know you."

"Then get to know *this*, honey!"

Loretta whipped out her schlong. Whipped it, wagged it,
then shook it firmly, the way she had seen men do when releas-
ing the last drops of urine after a nice long pee.

Sandra Thwaite-Barnside's eyes bulged.

"How about a blowjob, for old time's sake? We'll call it even."

The other woman recoiled. "Get away from me," she hissed.
"You're a sicko."

"I'm not a sicko. I'm a frustrated interior designer who just
discovered that she's got a schlong. And you know what? I like it.

It feels good having something between my legs. I haven't gotten my first hard-on yet, and I'll probably never have a set of balls to match, but I like my schlong. I'm proud of it."

"Good for you," Sandra said through clenched teeth. She tried to set her gaze forward, but her eyes kept wandering down to Loretta's schlong. Her cheeks were flushed. She was actually kind of pretty. Loretta imagined her on her knees, licking tentatively at the schlong, then gripping it hard as desire overcame her distaste.

Loretta could swear that she felt a bolt of sensation course through her pseudo-cock. The thing even seemed to stir a little in her palm, waking to the possibilities that its owner was envisioning. An array of tantalizing clichés drifted through her mind: throbbing meat, pulsing shaft, rampant member. What would it feel like to have a pair of soft, moist lips wrapped around her rampant member?

"Won't you at least consider it, Sandra? I promise not to take you to small claims court if you'll suck my dick."

Sandra Thwaite-Barnside shoved her shopping cart forward.

"It's not like I'm asking you to sleep with me!" Loretta called after her. "Oral sex isn't real sex, you know. It's not even considered infidelity anymore!"

The cashier at the deli counter gaped at Loretta. Loretta tucked her schlong back into her raincoat and gave the teenage boy an indulgent smile. She couldn't expect the average person to swallow the contradiction of her schlong. After all, Loretta was a pussycat of a woman, a sweet, curvaceous creature. Now she had a cock. She would have to give the world some time to get used to that paradox.

Having a dick made Loretta feel rich, broad, and full. Her large breasts, unconfined by a bra, rolled back and forth as she walked, and the schlong struck her thighs like a fuzzy pendulum with each step. She wasn't just some chick with a big banger; she was an androgynous pagan deity, a living symbol of fertility, male and female wrapped up in one juicy package. Loretta's body had turned into a totem. It deserved to be carved in the oldest of stones.

Slowly she paced in front of the deli display counter, surveying the cold cuts. Only the best would do for Loretta's schlong. Some people, like Tamara's fiancé, used their schlongs for evil—wielding them like weapons to break hearts, hymens, and engagements. Loretta would use hers for acts of transformation. She didn't know what shining deed she would perform with her schlong, but she could tell that the tube of flannel held a promise of miracles.

"I'd like to get that summer sausage, please. The whole thing," Loretta said.

The boy gawked at the sausage Loretta had selected. Its girth was probably nine inches, its length about eight. Wider than it was long, it fit Loretta to a tee.

"You want me to wrap it?" the cashier asked.

"Definitely not."

Loretta reached for the fragrant sausage. For a few moments she let it lie across her palms as she relished its smooth, oily texture, its solid heft.

"You can pay for it here," the boy offered. "So you could, uh, use it right away."

Loretta pulled a twenty-dollar bill out of her purse. While the cashier rang up her change, she unwound her schlong, wrapped the sausage in the flannel, and readjusted the elastic band. All this she performed with the delicacy of a surgical operation, while the cashier watched.

"How does it feel to have an erection?" Loretta asked.

The cashier pondered this for a second. "Pretty great, when

it's not embarrassing." He smiled. "Having a dick is a blast. I think you're gonna love it."

"I think I will, too."

• • •

Sometimes she dreamed that she was naked in the supermarket. Sometimes she dreamed that she was on a free shopping spree, piling her cart with imported chocolates and cheeses. But Loretta had never dreamed that she would be standing in front of the deli counter, performing a penile implant on herself with a sausage. Her dreams just weren't that weird.

As she walked back to her car, Loretta's schlong knocked against her thighs with an impressive weight. Each blow gave her goose pimples. She was so giddy with the strangeness of this hidden marvel that she couldn't decide where to go next. What did *men* do when they had a hard-on that wouldn't subside? Go to a strip club? An adult bookstore? Both of these scenarios left a rusty taste in Loretta's mouth. She had seen men masturbate, and they seemed to like it, but that didn't appeal to her, either. She wanted to share her schlong with someone. But with whom?

Loretta drove aimlessly through her neighborhood. With one hand she held the steering wheel, and with the other she stroked her schlong. Feeling predatory, she eyed the pedestrians on the sidewalk. Which one of them would like to see her brand-new prick? Maybe the elderly man walking his dachshund. Or the bouncy housewife wheeling a stroller.

A flash of light in the sky caught Loretta's attention. High above, a white helmet glittered in the spring sunshine. The man wearing the helmet was standing in the bucket of a truck parked beside a telephone pole. His tanned arms gleamed. Under the helmet Loretta saw sheaves of hair that might be blond, or gray.

Loretta's brakes squealed. Her tires scraped the curb as she stopped the car. The man at the top of the telephone pole looked down. Loretta jumped out of her vehicle. She stood on the sidewalk, threw back the panels of her raincoat, and held her prosthetic penis aloft. Her gathered nightgown rose up around her hips. A cool spring breeze frisked her thighs.

"How do you like my schlong *now?*" she shouted. The man gave Loretta a thumbs-up, then grabbed his own crotch.

"That's a hell of a thing you've got there," he called down. "Almost as big as mine."

Loretta's heart leaped. So did her schlong. "Want a closer look?"

"You bet!"

"I live in the little yellow house at the end of this block," she cried. "Come by when you're done if you want to check out my equipment!"

"Baby, I'll come anywhere you want me to. I'm off in an hour."

Back at home, Loretta prepared herself like a bride. Tenderly she set her member aside so that she could bathe, though she would have liked to see the schlong floating on a pillow of bubblebath. After her bath she put the schlong back on, only this time she left her breasts bare and wore the nightie like a holster, wrapped around her waist. She posed in front of the mirror, stroking her schlong, holding it upright, thrusting and parrying like a swordsman.

Men could do so many things with their dicks, Loretta thought wistfully. They could write their names with urine in the snow, make themselves erupt like Roman candles, even stir vats of warm chocolate pudding. For the first time in that magical afternoon, the phrase *penis envy* crossed Loretta's mind. Did she secretly want a penis of her own? A real one, with a glans, a urethra, a prostate—the whole shebang? Loretta dropped her schlong. The sheathed sausage dangled against her thigh. Her schlong had been a total surprise, something she had never wanted or expected to want. It had been a gift. How could you covet a gift?

As she was wiggling into her bathrobe, the doorbell chimed. Even those familiar tones sounded exotic on this bizarre day. Loretta hurried to open the door. The telephone man filled the threshold like a sun king, the late afternoon light fringing his silhouette in gold. He was taller, his shoulders broader, than she had realized. He cradled his helmet in his left hand. That hand looked wide enough to smother half of Loretta's bottom. Big hands, big dick—that's what she had always heard. She felt a tremor of defensiveness for her schlong. It wasn't Loretta's fault that she was small-boned.

"Hey," he said. "Remember me?"

I don't even know this guy, Loretta thought, veering toward sudden panic. Then she grasped her schlong, and that giddy, intoxicating confidence flooded back. All he wanted to do was check out her new hardware. If he made any scary moves, she could whack him with it.

"Of course. Won't you come in?"

"My name's Craig, by the way," the man said as he shouldered his way inside.

"I'm Loretta."

"Pretty name. Don't be nervous, Loretta, I'm not a psycho or anything. It's just that when I saw you with that fake dick in your lap this morning, it gave me a charge like I've never felt. I've been strapping wood all day. Mind if I sit down?"

Loretta waved him toward the sofa. "Go ahead. This has been such a crazy afternoon, I don't think anything would surprise me."

Craig smiled. His tanned cheeks looked leathery but soft. Buttery. His eyes were the color of semisweet chocolate chips, like the birthmarks that flecked his arms. If there was anything about this man that didn't remind Loretta of food, she hadn't seen it yet. He even smelled of nutmeg and campfire coffee, with a tangy note of fresh sweat.

"Sounds like you've had a hell of a day," Craig said. "Tell you what. Why don't you sit down, and I'll give you a blowjob. There's nothing as relaxing as a good hummer. Beats beer, pot, any substance known to man."

"Well! Well, well."

Loretta stumbled to the sofa and sank into the piles of throw pillows. Craig knelt in front of her. If she hadn't been able to sit, she would have collapsed where she stood. Her thighs quivered. Her pussy felt like a porcupine, bristling with anticipation. The schlong wobbled between her legs. She held the rod upright and pointed it in the direction of Craig's mouth. His lips, under their layer of chapped skin, were a tender pink. She wished he would kiss her before he sucked her schlong, but she was afraid to ask. She should feel grateful that he was willing to perform fellatio on her sausage. If she got too pushy, he might turn cold. He get mad and leave. He might even start to cry.

"How long have you worked for the phone company, Craig?" Loretta asked, in what she hoped was a cool tone. She really should find out more about him before he began to suck. He wasn't just a mouth, he was a man, with a personal history and a private life. She murmured soothingly as she reached for Craig's thick hair. It looked coarse, but it felt like corn silk.

"Eighteen years."

"What did you do before that?"

"Not a hell of a lot."

"What do you do in your time off?"

He grinned. "Pull on my pecker and dream about women like you."

Craig didn't seem concerned about sharing his personal history or his private life. His eyes were fixed on the flannel-covered sausage that Loretta held out to him. His nostrils quivered. The smell of spiced meat wafted up between Loretta's legs. Her stomach gurgled.

"Let's make this more interesting," Craig said. "Why don't you take off that bathrobe and unwrap that famous schlong?"

"Why should I unwrap it?" Loretta eyed Craig's teeth suspiciously. His canines were long and sharp, and the edges of his incisors were corrugated, like steak knives.

"Trust me. You'll like what I've got in mind."

Although she knew her lush body was beautiful, Loretta always felt a shudder of self-doubt at the moment she disrobed in front of a lover for the first time. What would Craig think about her ample breasts, with their wide pink nipples and lacing of silver stretch marks? What would he think of the rolls of her belly, the pouch of flesh that overlapped the top of her mons like a coy cap?

Today, however, with her schlong in hand, Loretta felt an entirely different hesitation. She didn't care about her breasts or her belly, only about the size of her newly acquired organ. Earlier Craig had boasted that his cock was bigger than Loretta's. When he saw Loretta's schlong without its pink flannel holster, he might burst out laughing.

That's no schlong! he would snort. *That ain't nothing but a meat stick!*

While Loretta unwrapped the sausage, Craig eased the bathrobe off her shoulders. He surveyed Loretta's body as if it were a steaming smorgasbord.

"Spread your legs, gorgeous," he said. His voice was husky. Loretta shivered. The chill didn't come from a draft. Craig took the sausage from her hands.

Loretta parted her thighs. Her labia made a kissing sound. Craig slid a forefinger into her vagina, gauging her wetness. Then he spread Loretta's lips, his hand acting like a wrench to open her, and inserted the end of the sausage. He worked it in a couple of inches, then sat back on his heels.

"Wait a second. This ain't right." Craig frowned at the schlong as if it were a broken tool.

"What's wrong?" Loretta's libido plunged. Craig was married. Or worse—he had suddenly realized that Loretta wasn't a goddess, just an insane woman with a sausage protruding from her vagina.

"Your dick's supposed to be sticking up, honey. See how it's pointing down, like a piss hard-on? I'd have to lie on my belly to suck that thing. We're gonna have to get you down on the floor."

Loretta could have wept with relief. He was right; her schlong was drooping at a dispirited angle. She removed the sausage and slid onto the floor. Craig stripped the sofa of its cushions and throw pillows and prepared a place for Loretta to recline. Half nest, half gynecological soft-sculpture, the pillow structure allowed her to lie back with her head and arms supported and her bottom elevated. Craig was a master craftsman; he had built an odalisque's bed. The cushions had been arranged to let her flesh flow like cream cascading over stones.

With his own member bulging in his faded jeans, Craig had to unbuckle his belt and undo a few buttons on his fly before he could kneel. He was gracious enough not to unveil his schlong completely—this, after all, was Loretta's moment.

"OK, baby. Let's try this one more time."

Loretta tilted her pelvis, and Craig inserted the sausage into her pussy once again. After a few moments of wriggling, she worked the wand into place. From this position, the schlong stretched her cunt to its limit. Loretta didn't think her vagina could stretch any further; still, Craig wasn't satisfied with the angle. He gripped one of her buttocks in each hand, lifted her hips, and gave the sausage one more slippery shove. Finally her schlong was standing tall.

"Now, this is perfect. You ready?"

Incapable of speech, Loretta nodded.

Craig lowered his head. In slow circles he swirled his tongue around the tip of Loretta's schlong. A deep hum of pleasure rose from his throat as he savored her meat. She could swear that she felt the texture of his tongue. When Craig shifted to a vertical lick—up and down, root to tip—Loretta closed her eyes in bliss. The sausage squeaked as it wedged its way into Loretta's body. There was something so magical, so mesmerizing about having a lover minister to you this way. No wonder men loved fellatio. You didn't have to do anything, just lie back and play with your lover's hair. Cunnilingus always made Loretta nervous; she worried that she was taking too long to come, that her lover would get lockjaw trying to pleasure her. But the schlong was just a sausage. The only thing she had to worry about was that Craig's after-work hunger might overpower his lust.

Craig's lips stretched skillfully around the shaft as he swallowed it, inch by inch. Loretta wondered if he had ever sucked another man, or if he were going on imagination alone. With the two ends of the sausage buried, it looked more than ever like a taut, ruddy erection rising out of Loretta's pubic curls. The sausage skin glistened. She touched the wet surface. Sparks shimmered through her body, and she moaned. She held the back of Craig's head, urging him to go further. He let her push him down, then he pulled back, then lowered his head again, his lips making succulent slurping sounds as they dragged up and down Loretta's schlong.

Did the heaviness in her pussy feel like the tightening of a man's balls before climax? A new expectation had seized Loretta, a growling, subterranean excitement that held a promise of fiery explosions, cascades of spume. She had always wondered what it would feel like to ejaculate, to grab the root of her dick and spray her seed in gleeful spurts. Craig was deep-throating her now. Her schlong was disappearing into his beautiful, leonine head. She thrust her hips, and the rocking motion brought the schlong in contact with her clit. As if to remind her of what she had neglected, the mighty pearl sent a spear of pleasure through her body, which lifted Loretta straight off the pillows into a stratosphere of soundless delight. She couldn't even hear herself screaming, though she felt the scream surging through her chest. With each throb of her orgasm, the schlong gave a slow, deliberate twitch.

Loretta was *sure* she ejaculated. Just because she never saw the product didn't mean it wasn't real; she had simply found a man who was gracious enough to swallow. Craig swallowed not only Loretta's invisible seed, but the tail end of her schlong after he bit it off in a frenzy of hunger. With each savage bite, Loretta felt that part of her flesh was being devoured, but it seemed like the right kind of sacrament to end the dream. After five or six chomps of Craig's big, corrugated teeth, half her schlong was gone. Before he finished, she made him give her the chewed end of the sausage as a memento of that strange afternoon.

"Damn, that did me good," he gasped. "That *changed* me, lady. Every time I get naked with a woman from now on, I'm gonna see her with tits, a pussy, and a dick rising up between thighs, and I'm gonna get down on my knees and blow her to kingdom come."

Loretta glowed. Craig kissed her. As their tongues intertwined, Loretta tasted spicy seasoning. Her schlong had changed the flavor of Craig's mouth. Loretta's stomach rumbled like thunder.

• • •

Weeks later, when she was having lunch with Tamara, Loretta decided to reveal the secret of the schlong. Even if that afternoon had been a dream, its promise was very real. Tamara was breaking up with Brad again. She would never be thin enough to wear his ring. But weeping wasn't going to heal Tamara's heart. What she needed was a schlong of her own, a tool to rival the one that Brad had been applying to women all over town.

A schlong wasn't merely a substitute penis, Loretta would inform her friend. It wasn't a weapon or a reproductive organ, but something in between, an instrument of creativity and transformation. Tamara would have to learn to move her entire body differently just to accommodate the sausage. She would have to stand up straight, thrust her voluptuous bosom forward, and let her hips sway in counterpoint to the swinging schlong.

"A woman with a schlong is a kind of superhero," Loretta would say, as she instructed her friend in the proper use of her new appendage. "She can use her power for evil, or she can use her power for good...."

OFFICE HOURS

Dawn Dougherty

It was when she walked away that she caught my attention.

She was a big, juicy woman and filled out her short black skirt with an ass that shook me out of my fog. She wore a pair of black heels, sheer nylons, and a standard white blouse that all deserved my undivided attention. But the only thing I could see as she walked away was that curvy, round ass. The way it swung from side to side, you would've thought there was an exclamation point on either side of her.

I had been moving my desk closer to the window when she knocked on my office door.

"Hi."

I looked up, startled to see someone standing there. The desk was dusty, and my hands were dark and sooty. Some of it had rubbed off on my pants.

"Hi," I said wiping my hands off.

"I work in Purchasing, down the hall," she smiled. "I just wanted to make sure that all the supplies you ordered came in."

I looked around my office for anything that remotely resembled office supplies. I spotted an official-looking box.

"I think everything's here," I said from behind my desk. "To be honest, I haven't even unpacked my own stuff yet." I wondered what my hair looked like.

"Oh, sure. Just let me know if you need anything." She had big brown eyes. "Actually, just fill out a supply request form and bring it down to our office." I nodded my head and said, "Thanks."

She turned to leave. "Nice to meet you—and welcome to the college."

"Thanks."

The whole exchange lasted less than two minutes, but the second she turned to walk away, everything slowed down. Like in a bad movie where the geek sees the girl of his dreams and she walks away in slow motion. Except I was a thirty-something dyke watching this sweet ass slide its way down the hall.

She turned at the end of the corridor and was out of sight, but I could still hear the echo of her clicking heels on the linoleum.

I went back to my office and sat down. I leaned back and imagined her sitting on top of my desk with her skirt hiked up. She'd have her legs spread wide open in front of me. I'd bury my head between her thighs, and she'd wrap her hands around my head and hold on. I'd take her in slowly, savoring each bite. She'd come and pull my face into her, digging her nails into the back of my head, and squeezing her thighs to my cheeks.

I licked my lips and could taste her.

"Well, how are you settling in?"

My boss's voice startled me out of my thoughts, and I went back to work.

• • •

I didn't see her again until two days later.

I had gone to the campus center cafeteria for lunch and passed her in line. I could smell her perfume as she walked by. I said hello and thought that she may have held my gaze a little longer than needed. I wasn't sure. She was wearing a pair of pants, but her ass still looked great. Round and full.

I got my lunch and sat at the opposite end of the cafeteria. I'd glance over at her table every so often. The front of her was as impressive as the back.

I figured that if I needed to, I could get her into my office again under the guise of a purchase order or something. She'd be in the black skirt from the day before, and as we talked I'd have her pushed up against the wall. I'd slowly unbutton her white blouse and pull out each of her tits. She'd moan and wrap one of her legs around my back and hook her heel into my belt loop. Then I'd push her back against the wall and suck on each one of her huge brown nipples until she begged me to fuck her.

Someone walked by and spilled a Coke on the floor next to me. It hit the ground and splattered all over my pants.

"Shit."

"Sorry, sorry, sorry," some nervous coed chirped. By the time I finished wiping off my pants she was gone.

• • •

The week passed quickly. I was busy getting settled and organized, and it wasn't until I was sitting in a two-hour new employee orientation that I saw her again.

I happened to look out the window as she was walking across the quad. Her whole body moved on cue when she walked.

First her breasts swung forward a little, and then each hip moved out to the sides, and finally her ass finished everything off. I *had* to meet this woman. This schoolboy fantasy bullshit was killing me. Maybe I was going through some sort of early midlife crisis. If I got a chance to do her again (assuming there'd be that first time), though, I'd have her on the couch in my office. She'd be on her stomach and I'd push her skirt up to her waist (I was really groovin' on the whole skirt thing). She'd arch up to meet me and I'd slide my tongue right in her ass. I'd spend hours just flicking my tongue in and out of her until she begged. Then I'd make her touch herself. She'd come right there on the couch, with my tongue up her ass and her fingers on her cunt.

The other new employees started to file out the door when I realized the orientation was over. I sighed and reluctantly headed back to my office.

• • •

We finally met up again the next day as we were both walking to the parking lot.

"Well, hello, stranger," she said. "I've been wondering how you were doing." She didn't look as if she had office supplies on her mind. But, given my state of hormonal imbalance I wasn't much of a judge.

"Really?" I said, trying to look inviting.

I'm sure we must have talked about something as we headed toward her car, but it could have been nuclear physics, for all I was concerned. I was lost thinking about the spots where her hair touched her neck and how the skin around her jaw moved when she talked. In fact it even took me a minute to realize she had her hand on top of mine. We had stopped and I was looking cool, leaning against her hood. I thought she was just going to pat the top of my hand, but she just left it there. My heart and clit jumped.

"It seems like I've seen you everywhere lately," she mused. The hand stayed.

"Uh-huh." I was sure I looked like an idiot.

As I was looking down at our hands, she slowly leaned in and kissed my neck right below my ear.

"I'm assuming you like girls," she whispered. I was thinking she was a little too sure of herself. She kissed me again, this time lower. "'Cause I do."

The only thing that kept me from thinking this wasn't just another fantasy was the silky feel of her lipstick coming off onto my skin. Like tattoos, she left her mark around my ear and neck and finally pressed herself onto my bone-dry lips. We kissed in the parking lot for a minute before I asked to take her home. She said she had a better place in mind and led me back into the building.

She headed toward my office, and when we got there she asked me to unlock my door. I couldn't remember which key was for what door or how I'd wanted to fuck her first. Was I gonna do her on the desk first, or the couch?

She was standing close behind me as I jingled the keys and felt her exhale. I was thinking about bending her over my desk when she reached around and grabbed my breast.

"Wait…" I said, as I finally got the door unlocked and we stumbled into my office. She had unbuttoned one of my buttons and was going for the second. This wasn't what I had in mind.

I turned around, took both of her hands, and tried pulling them behind her. She didn't budge. The momentum caught us both off balance, and we ended up slamming into the back of the door.

I thought I hurt her.

She smiled. "Don't fuck with me."

Before the words were out of her mouth, she had hooked her foot behind my heel and pushed my chest back. I fell flat on my back with a thud. She fucking tripped me! What a cheap god-damn trick. She was on top of me in an instant, sitting on my chest and pinning my elbows underneath her knees.

"I had five brothers," she said, looking down at me.

Definitely not what I had in mind. I had my hands up in a defensive posture, but instead of belting me one she pulled her sweater up over her head and threw it into the corner. Her large breasts fell out over the top of her bra.

"I'm in charge," she said as she stood up. "Or else I'm outta here."

Her tits were hypnotic. I lay my hands back down and nodded. I could like this.

She peeled her nylons off and then put her heels back on and sat down on top of my chest. I could really like this.

I lifted my chin and could see her dark pubic hair through the front of her skirt. She leaned forward and I dropped my head back.

"You wanna get under my skirt?"

She was a piece of work. She got up on her knees and hiked her skirt up to her waist. She was soaked. I reached up and finally got to squeeze that ass. I waited for her to lower herself on top of me. She hung out with her cunt inches from my face for what seemed like four hours. I strained my neck to get at her, until finally she lowered herself onto me and let her skirt drop. I parted her slick lips and practically devoured her in the dark-ness of her skirt. Her thighs squeezed my head and her heels pressed against my biceps as she rode my tongue and pressed herself down into my face. Her hips swayed back and forth and her hands dropped to the floor above my head as she moaned and ground herself into me. At some point my tongue lost the rhythm as she swiveled and circled her clit over my entire mouth. I moved my hands to her hips in a feeble attempted to rein her in, but she was gone. Her pubic bone pressed down on my lips and the soft fabric of her skirt pulled at my hair. She came with hot, jerky movements, her whole pussy pressed into my face.

When she finally stopped, she was on all fours. She pulled her cunt back from my face and then dropped just the tip of her clit back to my tongue. She left it, in an almost conciliatory gesture, for me to play with. Her breasts swayed back and forth as I sucked and pulled on her pearl-sized clit. She barely touched down, but my tongue and lips were happy for that little, tiny piece of her. She stayed, teasing me with her clit until her legs got tired. I thought maybe I could flip her and get at her ass, but she was done. She stood up and pulled her skirt down over her hips and thighs.

"This was good," she said as she buttoned up her shirt. She left her bra and nylons on the floor. I wondered if I was supposed to hold onto those for later. I was still flat on my back. "I may come back." Then she took the bottom of her foot and pressed it right on top of my clit and circled it three times. She stopped, gave me a smirk, and walked out. The last thing I saw from my view on the floor that night was her, her heels clicking on the linoleum, that big hot ass swinging from side to side down the hall.

THE MODEL

Catherine Lundoff

The sun broke through the clouds outside just as she turned her head, letting my lens catch her profile. The light trickled over the curtains of my dirty kitchen windows, spilling out over her with a golden glow. My hands shook a little. Maybe I should have done this in her apartment. Maybe I should have asked one of the others to be the first. One I didn't have a huge crush on.

I held the camera in front of me like a shield.

My pussy twitched and I had to force myself to keep the camera on her. I focused on the way her long, straight nose ran down to full lips and rounded chin. I wouldn't aim the lens to the ample curves below her jaw. Not yet. It had taken me weeks to work up the nerve to ask her to pose for me. I wanted to savor every minute of it.

She eyed me a little warily, like a shy cat. "Aren't you covering a lot of territory for a portrait?" she asked, head cocked to one side.

Not as much as I wanted to cover. I hadn't gotten her clothes off, for one thing.

The shutter clicked once, then again as I moved slightly to catch the blue gleam of her eyes, the reddish-brown sheen of her hair, buzzed Marine-short to show the shape of her head. I could feel my palms prickle at the thought of rubbing them over her skull.

"Well, I wanted to make this a well-rounded series. You know...like what our community leaders are really like. Serious shots and profiles and the reflective look and all that. Different angles...." I trailed off. Neither of us bothered to mention the nude shots. After all, I was doing a few of everybody, or so I said. Maybe I was. I couldn't remember what I'd told the others, not right now.

Sea-blue eyes studied me as I wiped one sweaty palm on my jeans. My self-confidence wavered under that look. What the hell was I thinking, anyway? She'd never go for another butch. Even a soft one. Even one who never looked at anything harder around the edges than a softball dyke before. For a minute, I missed the easy camaraderie of the beer and flirtation down at the Diamond, everyone's favorite post-game bar. It was so much simpler than this.

As I focused in on her again, I tried to remember her last girlfriend's name. Mimi? Cece? It was one of those real girly names. She even wore a dress to Jamie Anderson. It looked good on her, too, not as if she was doing amateur drag the way I did the few times I put on one of those things.

Still, I told myself, that girlfriend had been a few years back. Maybe she was looking for a change. Maybe that's all I wanted, too. I wasn't sure yet. I zoomed out to get a full view. She looked back at me fearlessly, and I let my gaze roam over her big, soft breasts and the round swell of her stomach. As my lens took in her whole body, she straightened up against the back of the chair and sucked her breath in slightly.

I lowered the camera in surprise. "It's OK, T. J. Just relax. The shot'll look better that way."

There was a soft hiss of air as she let her breath out, and I could see her blush a little when she looked up. The corner of her mouth twisted slightly, as if she wasn't too happy. I was getting worried.

"You wanna take a break?" The nude shots were starting to look like a bigger deal than I thought they would be. It hadn't occurred to me that she'd be uncomfortable.

She nodded at me and reached for the lemonade on the table, big solid hands grasping the pale blue glass until her fingers almost met around it. I tried to imagine those hands inside me as I watched the drink go down her throat in big gulps when she tilted her head back, draining the glass.

Imagining those fingers in other places—that was the easy part. Getting them there—now, that was another story.

My imagination took a little detour. Sure, she'd go for a butch who went for other butches. Who was I kidding? What'd the older dykes call it? "Kiki" or something like that. Hey, maybe I could just change my name. OK, so I was a little intimidated. It wasn't as if I'd done something like this before. Our eyes met as she lowered the glass to put it back on the table.

"So, how did you start doing photography, Kim?" Her voice matched the rest of her, deep but quiet. I always expected it to boom out of her, but somehow it never did.

"I took some classes down at the Y a couple of years ago. I liked it so much I took a couple more down at the tech college. Well, then you know how it goes, then Jane...you know Jane from the Center? Well, she saw some of my stuff and asked me to do a show. She suggested I do portraits of local lesbians. I'm kinda hoping it takes off, to see if I can quit my day job eventually."

T. J. nodded. "And Jane went for the nude shots? Seems kind of crazy for her." Her eyes crinkled up when she grinned.

Goddess, she even had a dimple!

My stomach flipped a little and my pussy went with it. I could feel my boxers getting a little damp. I tried to look casual as I pulled at my jeans to adjust them and kicked myself mentally a few times.

I am a butch. I am. I don't even know how to pick up another butch. Goody, a new mantra.

I finally noticed that she was waiting for an answer. "Huh? Oh yeah, well, it took some persuading. I told her it would bring in the kids and everybody's exes." Including my own, but the less said about that the better.

"I don't think I know any of your exes, Kim. Or your current lover. Are you seeing anyone?"

Not unless you counted the psycho bitch out in Oakvale who was sitting on half my stuff since she kicked me out three months ago. It wasn't much of a dating relationship at this point.

"No, my ex and I split a while ago. She lives outside of town." The one before her wasn't that great either. It wasn't much of a track record.

There must have been something in my face. "Ah," she offered. "Well, me neither. Hell of a town to be single in." She shook her head and gave me a mournful look. "Especially for an old warhorse like me. Cute young thing like you shouldn't have too much trouble when you're ready to start looking again."

Aaargh! She was talking about me as if I were a puppy. Hell, she wasn't that much older than I was—seven, eight years maybe. Time to change the topic. "So, what's with tensing up on that last shot? Is there something I can do or something you need to make you more comfortable?"

Like maybe a hot oil rubdown, or my face in your pussy?

I just couldn't say the thought out loud. Maybe I *was* a puppy. This was it: I was going back to the softball players this spring.

She studied the cracked green linoleum for a minute, one hand rubbing her stubbly hair as if she'd forgotten I was there. "Weeell," she said finally, "it's like this. I put on a lot of weight the last couple of years after I broke my leg and got sick and all, you know? I guess I'm just not as comfortable with it as I thought...."

Another light blush colored up her round, soft cheeks when she finally looked at me. I could feel my eyebrows shoot up. T. J. was a good, solid feminist dyke, pillar of the community and all that, and here she was stressing about her weight? Ick.

I decided that it was time for the careful approach. "Look, T. J., I think it looks good on you. Softens the edges, gives you more dignity."

Makes you hotter than hell, and I would personally volunteer to kiss and lick every extra curve.

My nipples hardened under my T-shirt at that happy little picture. I tried not to squirm. I could see her eyes wander down to my boobs. My pussy warmed to her look, spilling its warm wetness into my jeans. I made myself turn away for a minute. What the hell was she thinking about when she looked at me? Maybe I wasn't completely out of my mind after all. I fiddled with the camera for a minute before I turned back around, breathing real slow and casual, nipples pushed back in for the moment.

I *did* like the way she looked. The fat suited her, filled her out. Then I thought about what I said and how I said it. A moment of panic followed. Now she was probably worried that I had some kind of fetish and was out chubby chasing. Great. Her blue eyes studied me a minute longer. It was a look I couldn't read.

"Maybe you're right. Damn, I know you're right. I know better than this. It's just that...it feels so different. All of this."

She looked down at her big breasts and the rounded swell of her belly. I heard her take in a deep breath. "It's not like I think about it much except when someone's being a jerk. Or when a cute woman is pointing a scary little thing like that at me." Her gesture took in the camera, and I quivered a little at the flash of dimple and the second use of the word *cute*.

"Hell, if it'll make you more comfortable, T. J., I'll take off my clothes, too."

That didn't just come out of my mouth. No way. Oops.

She looked up at me again, this time with a twinkle in her eyes. Then her look ran down my body so slowly that I could almost feel her hands following. I couldn't believe I'd said it. The thought of being naked in front of her burned its way into my pussy, and I shivered. I'd be dropping the camera every five seconds when she looked at me. There was no way I could do this, but I wanted to. Oh God, did I want to!

It got really quiet, just the sound of our breathing and the hiss of the kettle for soundtrack. Her mouth quirked up in an amused half-smile and something else, something I couldn't read. Suddenly, she looked a lot more relaxed.

"Yeah, Kim, why don't you take your clothes off. In fact, why don't you give me the camera while you do it. I think that'd make me feel much more comfortable." She held out one big hand and our eyes locked. I swallowed hard. I've never been the dyke to ignore a challenge, not even this one.

I handed the camera over. She held it carefully while I showed her how it focused and one or two of its funny little habits. Then she nodded and just looked up at me with a little smile. I glanced over to make sure the curtains were closed all the way, then closed my eyes and just stood for a long moment.

"Not so easy on the other side, is it?" She said it softly, but it still pissed me off.

I could take my damn clothes off as well as she could. Maybe better. I backed up a few feet and opened my eyes. I glared defiantly at her while I yanked my T-shirt out of my jeans and tugged it over my head. The sports bra followed, and I was just starting on my belt buckle when she raised the camera and I heard the shutter snap. She got up and walked around me, catching me in profile.

"Slow down. This is kind of fun."

Goosebumps trailed up my bare skin, and I could see my nipples hardening into raisins at the touch of the air and the weight of her gaze. Suddenly, I wasn't pissed anymore. The butterflies in my stomach did a quick rumba when I looked back at the lens. I fumbled with my belt buckle, then tugged the belt slowly from the loops. Without even meaning to, I could feel my back arch a little, shoving my tits at the camera, at her. I raised one hand to run my fingers through my short-cropped hair.

"Hold it, supermodel. That's a nice angle." The shutter clicked again.

I could hear the purr in her voice now and couldn't resist pinching my right nipple a little, teasing it to a rigid point. Maybe this wasn't such a bad idea after all. I shivered a little and imagined her going down on me.

With my eyes closed, I popped open the button on my jeans and slid the zipper slowly down. I heard the camera again as I slipped them off over my hips, tugging my boxers with them. I opened my eyes again to find that she was snapping a shot of my profile. Out of the corner of my eye, I could see her lower the camera, and I turned to look back at her with my right hand on my hip, posing as I kicked my clothes away.

She looked interested, which was a relief. Glancing down, I wondered for a second if she was seeing the same body I was.

The one I saw was on the long and lean side, including some muscles, a couple of tattoos, and not much by way of boobs. It was nothing spectacular, but she was still looking when I checked again. I tried to figure out what to do next.

It got uncomfortable after a minute. I decided I wanted to be on the other side of the camera again. I tried not to feel quite so naked as I walked over to her, using my best swagger. The moist-earth scent of my pussy rose like a fog around us.

She examined me, nervously licking her lips. I held out my hand for the camera. Her blue eyes met my brown ones and I fell in, drowning in a warm sea. Which was how I came to be kissing her. It took a minute for her to kiss back. Then, slowly, carefully, her lips softened and opened against mine. My tongue flicked against them, inching its way gingerly into her mouth.

That was when she pulled back. "I'm not ready yet. It's been a while," she said. "I don't usually hop into bed with the first cute woman who waves a camera at me, you know."

She grinned at me so that I wouldn't feel too bad. I gave myself a sharp mental kick anyway. "Besides, a deal's a deal. I said I'd pose for you, and I'm a woman of my word."

It took me a minute to realize that the camera was in my hands again. She gave me a little smile and stood up. I stepped back, forcing myself to try to ignore the moist ache of my pussy. At least she wasn't leaving. And she hadn't said *no* in a permanent, "forever" kind of way.

She met my eyes and started pulling her T-shirt out of her jeans. I waited until she was tugging it off over her head before I snapped the shot. The sound echoed in the room and she froze for a second, arms wrapped in the shirt, face hidden. I could see the big, round curves of her breasts resting in a tight white bra. Soft, cream-colored skin rolled out over her belt. I wondered if it felt as silky as it looked. She finished pulling her shirt off.

I walked around her as she unhooked her bra, snapping a profile shot of her face and one muscular arm with its fading tattoo. She reached around to unhook her bra and stopped. My eyes met hers as I lowered the camera.

Her expression turned serious. "So, Kim, I still don't understand why you asked me to pose. What do you see when you look at me?"

The question threw me for a loop. Would she take off and never talk to me again if I answered wrong? What would answering wrong *be?* I didn't know. She just kept on looking at me and waiting.

"Um...well, I don't know. OK, OK, don't look at me like that. It's just an expression. I see...a dyke who I really admire. You remember that plumbing workshop you did at the Center? For me, that was what being a dyke was all about."

T. J. gave me the most horrified look I had ever seen. "That's quite a burden."

"No, no, hear me out. I got to sit there watching and listening to this strong, knowledgeable woman talk about something I knew nothing, and I mean nothing, about. And you made it seem easy. I remember watching you and wondering what you were like. Hell, I'm *still* wondering."

As an afterthought, I asked a question of my own. "Why did you agree to pose for me?"

I decided to stop while I was still ahead. Or was it behind?

"Wow." She looked down at the rug and shook her head for a minute. "That wasn't what I was expecting."

She pulled her bra straps down her shoulders almost as if she didn't know they were still there. I wondered if I'd passed the test, and I raised the camera to find out. Or at least capture the moment.

The shutter clicked just as her bra came off, and she looked up. She pulled her hands through the straps as if she was in a trance. Her breasts spilled out onto the round swell of her belly. I wanted to run my tongue over her raspberry nipples and cup them in my palms.

I opened my mouth. "You're beautiful," was what came out.

We stood there and looked at each other for a few minutes. She gave me a strange look, almost puzzled. Her eyes traveled over me, working their way down, then wandered back up to meet my own. Now they gleamed appreciatively. I knew it was going to happen then; it was just a matter of who would make the first move. I guess I knew that, too, but I wanted there to be some doubt, for the sake of my pride.

"I agreed to pose because I thought it would help me accept how I look now. And because I thought it would be a great thing to be a part of. It's pretty flattering to be asked to do something like this, you know. And because…" She hesitated a moment, then reached out and pulled me up to her, winding her solid arms around my waist, "…you are, too."

This time she kissed me back, her tongue slipping into my mouth and twisting together with my own. Awkwardly, I reached past her to put the camera down on the table.

Her hands started exploring, slowly and cautiously, stroking my back and then cupping one of my mouthful-sized breasts. I slipped my hands under hers like I had just imagined doing, and pulled away from her mouth to nibble my way down her neck to her nipples. Her moan seemed to roll up from deep inside, as if it hadn't had a way out for a while.

I slid my hand between her round, hard thighs and teased my way along the inseam of her jeans. Her legs parted slightly for my fingers, but I could feel her hesitate a little.

I stopped and looked up, giving her my best seductive grin. "You know, I've never done it with another butch. I don't know all the rules."

"Yeah, well, me neither, but I think we're both kinda soft in the rules department. I'm looking forward to finding out just how butch you are."

She was breathing a little harder. I lay my face against her big belly for a moment just to feel the rise and fall of it. My arms circled her waist, resting on the wide curve of her hips, until she tugged me upward to kiss me again. This time, her lips were hard against mine, and her mouth felt hungry, devouring my tongue. My pussy was groaning for the touch of her hand. Suddenly, I didn't really care how butch I was. Still, I couldn't help making a move to pull her toward the welcoming rectangle of my bedroom door.

She pulled back. "Don't you want to see the rest of the show? I still haven't taken my pants off for the West Coast audience. Besides, I like the look you've been giving me for the last hour. I want to see it for a little while longer."

My jaw dropped. I stood back with an effort as she walked slowly to the center of the room. My hand wandered over to the camera as if it had a life of its own. She started to unbuckle her belt. This time, she seemed to know what to expect. Her eyes sparkled as she met the lens, and she threw her shoulders back proudly as she gently tugged the belt from its loops.

One big hand started opening the button on her jeans and then unzipping her fly. The other rested on her hip as the shutter clicked. If she'd been packing, we could have sent that one to *On Our Backs*. I said it out loud and she grinned at me, chuckling a little.

Maybe next time. But I didn't say it. No point in sounding too eager.

The jeans dropped awkwardly off her round hips as she pulled them down to reveal the inevitable boxers. I suddenly wished I'd been wearing something frilly under my own jeans, both for the shock value and the sexy feel of rayon against my skin. After all, this was a special occasion.

Maybe next time for that, too. If there was a next time.

She kicked her pants aside and stopped, hands on the waistband of the boxers. I lowered the camera and grinned at her. It felt as if it split my face open. I wondered how hard I'd been trying.

She grinned back and yanked the boxers down. When she straightened up, I raised the camera for a quick shot. I wanted this one to turn out—this portrait of her standing with her legs apart, round soft belly edged with dark brown hair, big breasts with their dark nipples begging to be sucked. Her blue eyes twinkled, and I put the camera down and walked over to her.

"How do you feel?" I asked. For an answer, she placed her hands on either side of my jaw and kissed me hard.

When we stopped for a breather, she muttered, "Got a bedroom?"

"And plastic wrap. And gloves."

She grabbed my hand and pulled me toward the welcoming dark of the bedroom doorway. "Bring the camera. I can think of a shot I want for my wall."

BREATHING LESSONS

Eleanor Brown

Standing behind me, he pulls my sweater off my shoulders. His lips brush across the back of my neck, a whisper, a shiver, a promise. His hands slide over the arch of my shoulders, down to my biceps. I freeze, hold my breath. Tension skims through my veins. This is the moment when he will pull back, as his fingertips find the loose skin on my arms, the ripples where there should be muscle. He kneads, his hands slightly rough against the smooth softness of my skin. Although his hands are broad, he cannot circle my arms, and I know this is the moment it will end.

"Breathe," he whispers, his breath a hot semaphore against my ear.

I breathe.

Our older sisters possess secrets we do not. It is what keeps them thin. Their stomachs fade flat into their jeans, shirts tucked neatly. They have boyfriends. We watch them as they talk, the muscles on their forearms rippling with the slightest motion of a finger. We will not have men like that.

We try on our sisters' clothes, sneaking into their closets and exploring mysteries. Their dresses look strange on us, stretched the wrong way over puberty and baby fat, exposing pudges and ripples we did not know existed.

In their dresser drawers we find packets of Dexatrim. We turn the pills over and over, watching the tiny colored beads spill over and into each other. We put the package back where we found it. We remember.

We kiss, and I relax into terra firma. His body presses against mine, muscles long and lean, sleek like a racehorse. Where he is solid, I am soft, and I recoil slightly. His hands move down my back, skimming shoulder blades. I feel his erection pulsing against my stomach, and as his hands reach the base of my spine, I wait for it to deflate. He flattens his palms over the swell of my bottom, the flesh overflowing his fingers as he squeezes. I stiffen, my body a frozen live wire. My heart beats a rhythm between my thighs.

His mouth moves lower, tracing my collarbone, drawing infinity over the two tiny bumps beneath my skin. His hands clutch again, pulling me closer, molding my flesh to his touch. I meet his lines with my curves. "Breathe," he whispers.

I breathe.

We listen to the hush of hubbub in the mall, our mothers and us. All around us, there is a giddy buzz and the steady clink of cash registers. Our fingers trail along a cool store window, leaving a dim smudge along the sightline. Inside the store, there are girls our age, their fingers exploring the outfits behind the glass. We look at them sadly and we slink into a corner, to the store where the clothes will fit us.

Our mothers sit on a step, chin in hand, as we stand inside the dressing room, facing ourselves in the mirror. Our thighs bulge too high. We turn away, feeling the scratch of the fabric riding up between our legs, and we hate ourselves in silent wonder. We recall a million promises made between the pages of magazines. Broken pieces of failure surround us on the stained carpet.

Our mothers' eyes are joyless as they surrender their credit cards to clothe their fat daughters.

One-handed, he unhooks my bra, and it falls to the floor. My hands move automatically to my breasts, holding them up. The underwire has left telltale curves underneath them, sprays of broken blood vessels haunt my shoulders in spindly flowers. He pushes my hands away gently, and my breasts fall heavily against my chest, the nipples pointing toward the ground. Small silver streaks fall like frozen raindrops against the cream of my skin.

His hands replace mine, cupping and stroking, teasing my nipples into ripe raspberries. My skin is all over goose bumps, shivering up my arms and back down my thighs, making me tremble in places where before I have only ached. My breasts ooze over his palms, weak, shivering, Jell-O. I turn my head away, I cannot look. The rise and fall of my chest ceases, I bite my lip.

"Breathe," he whispers, air sliding over my damp skin, pulling my nipples taut as his mouth moves across my rib cage. He gently moves my face back, and I watch his mouth moving over my breasts, his mouth dark against me. His teeth graze my nipple, and I shiver in pleasure at the sight of gleaming white against the swollen pink.

I breathe.

Tracey goes away every summer and comes back thinner. She confides in us one night, when we are huddled inside sleeping bags, picking out the brown M&Ms. Her parents send her to fat camp. She eats cornflakes and broccoli for weeks on end, and plays sports all day. Tracey is an artist, and we cannot imagine her playing sports.

"Do you like it?" someone asks. We go to traditional summer camps, with arts and crafts, and canoeing.

Tracey shrugs. She doesn't know anything else. She has been going since she was ten. The camp is in a small town. When they walk back from the movie theater, a group of boys are standing at the end of an alley. They are silhouetted in the darkness, their legs spread wide in teenage bravado. They bark, they howl, like wolves braying at the moon.

Tracey tells us that she cries herself to sleep there, spreading herself out across the bed so that she does not have to touch her own body.

No one says anything.

His hands move over my stomach, tracing the relief map of my stretch marks, tree limbs reaching up, pale as morning light across the swell of my belly. This is the worst part, and though he has forged on before, I cannot imagine that he will continue through this. He reads my body like Braille, fingertips traveling lightly over the pebbles of flesh. His hand rests on my stomach, the heel brushing against the curls of hair above my thighs, his fingers pointing toward my face. My eyes are clenched shut, my fingernails making half-moons inside my palms.

I open my eyes, brace myself for the inevitable. He removes his hand, places it instead on either side of my stomach, his fingers arching out to accommodate the indentation of my waist, the soft ripples along my sides. I watch as he leans forward and presses the softest of kisses on my stomach. He looks up at me, his face framed by the drops of my breasts.

"Breathe," he whispers. I look at him, his face pressed against my stomach, and I push my hands through his hair. My nipples brush over his forehead as his tongue traces my stretch marks, his hands hold me on either side, and I do not shy away.

I breathe.

Somewhere along the way, we learn to believe that bigger clothes will make us look smaller. We are swathed in yards of fabric, shirts billow around us like sails, never tucked in. Somewhere there is the curve of a thigh, the arch of a back, the swell of a breast. You will not see it.

There are exceptions to the rule, of course: We can wear leggings if our shirt is big enough, but our stomachs must be hidden. Our bellies are full of shame, the way they curve as though they harbor a child. The twitch of our asses, the sway of our hips hidden by the sag of fabric.

We are swimming together, T-shirts floating around us like the legs of an octopus. "Marco," someone shouts.

"Polo!" we answer, swim away. There are girls in bikinis on the edge of the pool, and we dive underwater, holding our eyes open against the chlorine. Resurface, sputtering. When we climb out, our fists clutch at the hem of the shirt, pulling it low over our thighs. We scurry for towels.

Yes right here oh please oh please oh please.

His hand is moving slowly, creeping like a centipede. I part my thighs for him as his fingers slide over wet folds. His hands are like pincers, tugging at the moist lips. His thumb finds my clit, circles it, draws back. I gasp in pleasure, push down against him. "More," I whisper. "More."

He complies, moving his thumb against me again. A warm trickle slips from his hand over my thigh. He moves down to kiss it away, his tongue dangerously close to his hand. His lips brush my thigh, and I pull up slightly, condensing the spread of my leg. My feet flex automatically, bringing my body under control, holding myself still so that I will not quiver.

Instead of pulling away when his tongue brushes across the pliant, pale skin of my thigh, he kisses it again. My muscles strain from the tension, beg for release. He pushes a finger inside me, firm, presses down on my thigh with his other hand, my flesh pushing out against the bed like cookie dough.

"Breathe," he whispers, and his breath slides inside me along with his finger. He presses up lightly and I gasp, my hips moving involuntarily to meet him. My toes point, my thighs flatten against the bed. I spread wide for him. For me.

I breathe.

Lisa is dating a new man, a tattoo artist. He has drawn a small star above her heart in ink, and we all whisper that it will not last. We don't think much of him, his elegant hands on darkly painted arms. Lisa thinks he is dangerous, and as we see her shrinking inside herself, hiding her stomach when she turns to change her shirt, we agree.

"He says I'd be prettier if I were thin," Lisa confides in us. We eye his beer belly suspiciously.

She smokes a lot, drinks coffee, buys the Cindy Crawford workout video. In the mornings, when she comes home from his bed, her face is tearstained. "He made me heart-shaped pancakes," she says, as though that explains everything. We say, "Oh."

The beauty that is the convex curve of Lisa's stomach disappears into vapid flatness. She smiles less, smokes more. She goes out with him instead of us. She gives us the clothes she is too thin for, but our arms stretch the fabric of the sleeves so we throw them away. We miss her.

His mouth is pressed against me now, he is tasting me, his tongue exploring crevices and curves. I cannot relax, I cannot move, I cannot surrender. But he does not stop, he moves one arm up, creeping its way back up over my stomach, slipping up to toy with my breasts. I press my arms against my sides to stop the avalanche, and my nipples dimple in.

He pinches my left nipple, hard, his arm still lying flat across my body. I hold my breath, feeling that he is inside me, around me, all over me, all at once. If I lie still, he will not notice. His tongue moves inside me, wiggles pleasantly, slides back out. The slight scratch of his stubble makes me tremble against my will, his chin slipping inside me.

I am shaking now, my thighs trembling in pleasure. I am drowning in his tongue, and I push down against him, feeling the weight of his arm against my stomach. He moves his mouth back to meet me, suckling gently as a shudder creeps from my toes up my legs, and then it rolls over me in a hot wave and my thighs squeeze his head tight, spreading unapologetically as I burst like ripe berries in his mouth.

He pulls his hand back, pushes up and looks at me. His skin glows dark above me, his muscles carved from marble as he holds himself up. "Breathe," he says.

I breathe.

For Melissa's birthday, we go dancing. Steam rises from the dance floor, the beat vibrates in our chests. We move onto the floor, swing, sway. Our bodies are rich with rhythm. Melissa does a slow undulation as she turns, her eyes closed in pleasure. She looks around, sees the men leaning against the bar, shirts tight against their chests. The women wear short skirts, platform shoes.

As we dance, we watch. Men lean in, whisper in women's ears. Women laugh, toss their hair back over their shoulders. Melissa moves back, brushes against someone. He turns, smiles, they dance together. We admire they way their bodies move. Melissa has always been the best dancer. Her legs move easily, her arms twist through air like water.

He moves closer, the muscles in his thighs taut under his jeans. Melissa's full breasts brush against his chest, her eyes heavy-lidded with the lust of dancing. Lights spin, swirl, paint our faces bright and then dark again. They look good together, tight lines against loose curves. Sweat stains her forehead, slips like a signal between her breasts.

Later, we hear him with his friends at the bar. "Who was the fat chick you were dancing with?" He shrugs, grins. We turn away.

When he moves inside me, I open for him, blooming pink flesh around him. His eyes close for a moment and then open again, darkening skies. "God, you are beautiful," he whispers. His head ducks down and he captures a nipple in his mouth, tugging at it. I move my hands away from my sides, letting my breasts spill down, splay my palms out over his back, the heat of his skin branding me.

We push together, apart, I feel the muscles in his back rippling with each thrust. His hand slides down between us, and I suck in my stomach. He frowns, pulls me over, still hard inside me. I am on top, my breasts sway slightly as he grabs my hips, pulls me forward. His fingers intertwine with my flesh, pressing out where he presses in.

He tries again, moves his hand under the fall of my stomach, finds my clit. He rubs it, and I shiver in pleasure. He smiles, keeping one hand on my hip, he guides my movements. I am lost, shivers of sweat trickle down my body as we move, faster and faster. His fingers draw concentric circles around my clit, a spiral drawing me up.

I am aware for a moment of the sound my stomach makes as I drive down, pulling him deeper inside me, uncorking him like wine. It slaps against him, ball into mitt, and I inhale, pulling it back into me, but then he tweaks my clit again and I forget, I explode. My body trembles and then shakes, a tremor spreading both up and down, making every inch of my flesh shiver.

"Beautiful," he whispers again. He thrusts up to meet me, his hand still squeezing my hip, and I glance down to see my flesh overflowing his hand. I pause, he draws another slow circle with his finger, and I shoot over the edge like a star, clutching at him inside and out. He meets me, I feel him pulse inside me, hard inside soft, hard against soft.

He pulls me down, kisses me hard, and I relax in his arms, my body spreading out over his in soft ripples like cake batter. His hands trail lightly down my back and I kiss him again.

I breathe.

MÄDCHEN IN UNIFORM

Heather Corinna

"I couldn't put my finger on it when we met, but there was something about her. Her coloring was beautiful—that swarthy, European-peasant sort with sun-burnished skin, very striking blue eyes, and hair the color of burnt sienna with honey streaming down it in waves."

"She sounds a lot like me."

"Very much so. Anyway, she liked being outdoors, spent a lot of time on the beach smoking joints and watching the waves. But that wasn't what the 'something' was. I liked her a lot, even though we didn't know each other very well. Being around her made me feel very fun, but very safe and cared for at the same time. Some of that was simply her, who she was. Much of it was her build, and I know that sounds shallow. There's all those goings-on about how a book shouldn't be judged by its cover, but in her case, she just got an excellent designer: Her cover was the perfect match for her book.

"Probably when she was growing up, people would have called her 'a big girl,' or maybe 'chubby,' if they were feeling nice, and even then, they'd have said it behind her back. Others may have just said she was *fat,* but that word, for me, never fit her; never even occurred to me. It wasn't about political correctness, it was about language as it is supposed to be: accurate description.

"It was as simple as this: Her body and spirit were designed for *Trachten,* real honest-to-God German peasant clothes. You know, dirndls, and poofy white blouses, and those German vests—the tight ones with the silver buttons, the leather ones. She just looked the part. She was tall, and as solid as an oak tree, but her rounded cheeks and fleshy bosom begged, pleaded even, to bloom atop an embroidered bodice, her thick, sturdy calves stemming a full skirt that illustrated her wide, florid hips and that gorgeously rounded bottom. *Willkomen,* my wet dream.

"I knew all of that from the moment we met, though I wouldn't have been able to discern it for a while. It wasn't that she didn't look divine in her worn Birkenstocks, her fraying cutoff shorts, and her torn T-shirts, because she did. But they just didn't illustrate the goddess that she was, and no matter what she was wearing, in my mind, I would see her at bosom's-eye-view, lace peeking from her bodice, and a jolly light in her eyes, in the middle of some noisy, small-town *Biergarten.*

"It all sounds so perverse. It probably is, and in telling it to you, it sounds that way, but in my mind's eye, it is homage, it is glorious, it is the only way to describe her."

"You sound jealous," she said. "Hell, *I'm* jealous."

"Oh, I was. I was—and still am—terribly, painfully jealous, and it's a serious ache to both want someone as well as want to *be* someone. Even if I'd gained a hundred pounds I couldn't have been her. It isn't about the weight. Why do people always think it's about the weight? I couldn't just gain some and be her, you know. It was how she carried it, it was how it embellished her. I couldn't carry an orange as well as she carried herself."

"So what did you do?"

"For a long time, nothing. We went out to parties now and then together; we were casual friends, not close, we didn't share secrets or tragedies, or anything like that, but we had a good time. She liked men, though. I liked her. So, you see, we had what you'd call a bit of a conflict."

"So, it was unrequited? Nothing ever happened? Or did she come around? I did, you know, and we were like that at first...."

"Yes, you did. I didn't say it was unrequited—did I say that? Oh, something certainly happened.

"We were out one night, party-hopping, one to the other, in the rich neighborhoods north of Chicago. We were both college students, but not the kind who had empty mansions to come home to on weekends: We waitressed at night to pay for our schools, and lived in apartments where the roaches hogged the covers at night. Although we'd both grown up just on the other side of the suburbs in the city, we had made friends, ex-lovers, and the lot over the years in richer circles. Of course, we felt a bit like infidels, invaders, but that was part of the fun of it.

"It was a strange dynamic we had, and I'm not sure I can describe it very well. She and I would go out, and everywhere we went, the men and women would stare at me, flirt with me, ask to take me home, but they would smile tentatively at her, only talk to her briefly, but keep a distance. All the while, I was the one who felt like the ugly stepsister beside her, a stunted, ridiculous clod compared to her queenly, voluptuous grace. I felt like an impostor, really, as if somehow my body or my face made me look the most attractive, while meanwhile hers was hiding who the real beauty was.

"In any event, we'd gotten bored at one of the parties, and were sneaking through the rooms, our heads dizzy with pot and booze. She had found a suite with its own bath, and we'd holed up with our tidy stash and she—effusive as always—had drawn herself a bubble bath and hopped in enthusiastically, dragging me in beside her, as I struggled to get my clothes off before I ended up in the water head first."

"That must have been horrible for you."

"Oh, honey, it was nothing close to horrible. Horrible comes later. Stop interrupting and I'll get there.

"Horrible is *not* when the woman of your dreams is sitting across from you, covered in mounds of bubbles, skin glistening with drops of water, and sweat beading on her face. That is divine, no matter what happens. She was full-out drunk, to boot, and kept telling me how beautiful I was, kneading my feet, rubbing my calves, poking at my nipples like a little girl. I told her then she was a goddess and she laughed. She didn't believe me, said I was drunk, and I assured her that while that was certainly the case, I thought as much when sober. She still didn't believe me.

"So I kissed her. She only held back for a minute, and then returned it back, fully. I got to slide my hands up her wet sides, my lips over nipples larger than my lips, and sank my fingers into those delicious thighs. I can't begin to describe to you the sensation of it all. Coupled with the near-to-boiling water, my twat felt insanely warm, and if I had even been just a little more drunk, I surely would have eaten her up from tits to toes."

"So, it *was* consummated...oh, yum."

"Hush up, you're interrupting again. As I was saying, there I was, literally bathing in this woman, one hand hungrily cradling a plump cheek, the other between her thighs. I slid my thumb between her lips and she squirmed and cooed like a dove as I circled her clit with it, slipping my fingers inside her and started to pump her slowly, as I locked my lips unto one of her nipples, sucking insistently like an infant."

"This is getting *good.*"

"Then she jumped up, grabbed a towel, and shot across the room."

"What the hell? What's with that? Did she get scared?"

"Hardly. She got hungry, is what she got. She started squealing about how horny I'd made her, and started diving through the closets there looking for something to wear as I made my way out of the tub and grudgingly put my clothes back on. I came out of the room, and there she was, doubled over in laughter in the closet, pressing herself into a costume she'd found squirreled away in the back."

"Oh, no, it wasn't..."

"It was. Exactly. A long blue dirndl, acres of white petticoats, a fine white blouse with embroidery and lace that would've made Liberace faint with envy. Oh please, would I make that up? There was even a *Mieder*...I knew I'd remember what they're called!...the leather vest with the metal buttons. Stop laughing at me! I was beyond myself with lust and longing. I know that sounds very Jackie Collins, but it's the best I can do. It gets worse, though."

"It does? Jesus."

"So anyway, still laughing, she pulled her hair into two thick braids, asked me to button up the bodice—which I did, making it last and screaming inside with frustration. She pushed her breasts hurriedly down into the costume and peeled down the stairs as the whole vision, in just a moment, had burned itself into my eyes and snapped, crackled, and popped, honey, between my legs. Then the worst thing happened.

"She fell? Oh God, that's so..."

"No, no, she didn't fall. When she got downstairs, everyone stopped. Just stopped dead in their tracks. Some of them laughed a little, some laughed a lot, but eventually it died down and turned into a very quiet, seductive awe. And then—oh, then—every last person in the house began circling around her: talking, flirting, and some saying absolutely nothing because they just couldn't. They were spellbound. I was right, see: It was really what she was meant to be wearing. I came down, and I was absolutely invisible to everyone else. Invisible, and frustrated as hell with a half-cocked clit, no less. They saw what I had all along, the blinders were off."

"So, what happened?"

"There was an orgy, eventually."

"What!? You've got to be kidding!"

"OK, so there wasn't an orgy. She ended up picking up two different men, we all went down to the beach, and I watched them undo that lovely bodice from afar, and lose themselves in that incredible body one at a time while she cooed and sighed and moaned to the heavens. I sat by myself with my hand in my pants, alleviating my frustration with two fingers and my imagination."

"OK, so that *is* horrible."

"Oh, not really. I *did* see her the way I wanted to see her, I *did* get to indulge somewhat in what I wanted to, and I got to imagine the rest. The only thing that would have been better, of course, was if I had got to do what I wanted with her completely."

"So that's why you bought me this stupid outfit?"

"That's why I bought you that outfit, and it's not stupid. You'll look divine in it, I promise."

"What was her name, anyway?"

"Moira."

"How weird! She looked like me *and* she had my name, how—*oh, you little shit!* That story isn't even true, is it?"

"No. But it could be, no? Get dressed, my gorgeous, gullible *schöne Fräulein*. I'll draw us a bath."

WEEKDAYS AT ROSINI'S BAKERY

Veronica Kelly

I'm a thirty-two-year-old single woman and I live in an old, working-class neighborhood in Pittsburgh, just a few blocks from the best bakery and coffee shop in town, Rosini's Bakery. Early in the morning before I head to my job downtown, I like to go there and sit at one of the old mahogany café tables, sip that strong coffee, and gaze out the window to the tree-lined street, sampling one of their doughy confections.

One cold November morning, I sat at my usual table at Rosini's and watched customers trample the wooden floor, worn bare in the middle of the shop where customers have walked in and out for the past forty years. The walls of Rosini's are covered in a thick coat of pale-green enamel paint, and the white tin ceiling is ornate enough to pass for another one of the fancy pastries under Rosini's glass counter. That morning, I'd dressed with Mr. Rosini in mind—Vincent Rosini, the owner of the bakery—a man with brown eyes so bright they could belong to a thirty-year-old, not a seventy-year-old, and a large, wide mouth that tends to curve up into a whimsical smile, a nice complement to his skin, an olive tone that makes him look sun-kissed year round. He isn't particularly tall, nor is he portly, despite what you might assume for a man whose life has been pastries and coffee for the past forty years. You might say I found him attractive, and he seemed to like to look at me, so that day, I put on an outfit just for him: black velvet skirt that fits tight around my well-fed ass, hips, thighs, and tummy, and a fuchsia sweater with a plunging neckline. In clothes like that, I always feel like an exotic flower against the cold, gray Pittsburgh sky.

I sat there that morning, a Long John and a mug of coffee with two creams and two sugars on the table in front of me. Mr. Rosini's rich, homemade custard oozed out both ends of the Long John as I contemplated which end to bite into first.

"You haven't touched your treat," said a quiet voice. I looked up. Mr. Rosini stood at my table, wrinkled hands on his hips. I smiled up at him and met his gaze. He carried a tray with half-empty coffee cups, wadded paper napkins, and plates covered with crumbs.

"I've been enjoying the morning," I said as I ran my finger around the rim of the white coffee cup, wiping off a smudge of my pink lipstick.

"Mmm," he replied and smiled, looking out the front window to the street. It was 7:00 A.M. and the shop had been open for half an hour. "This is a good thing, to enjoy the morning." Several customers rambled through the front door, and Mr. Rosini walked back behind the counter to join his son, Ed, fetching treats and caffeine for the newcomers.

By 10:00 I had thrown a black blazer over my vivid, low-cut sweater and was in the throes of my job as a legal assistant for a

law firm. The jacket was buttoned to my neck and the hemline
fell below my hips, giving me a "leaner line," as the fashion magazines say. Everything about my job seems to be about being
lean, linear. We are encased in a concrete and glass box that is
twenty stories high. The carpets are beige, the light fixtures are
recessed. We wear black, navy, beige, or brown clothing. Our
hair is trimmed with precision. My thick, unruly locks are always
pulled back in a bun. I wear small glasses.

I know I'm not quite like the other office workers. I am not
sleek enough, nor is my hair coiffed. By noon, fuzzy strands
break free from the bun in my hair and dance down my neck. I
am dark and heavy and I wear makeup to hide my flaws. The
female attorneys are slim and blond, and their skin is like porcelain. Over lunch, when I go to the department store to browse,
it's the same thing. I see clothing made for *Ally McBeal*
wannabes, and get accosted by twenty-year-old sales clerks who
must spend their entire paychecks on clothing and makeup,
because they're most certainly not spending them on food.

None of those department store girls would be caught dead
eating custard-filled pastries for breakfast, that's for sure, I mused
to myself that afternoon while rebooting my cantankerous computer. I thought of the fat Long John I'd eaten, and how sensual I
felt sitting there with my breasts straining up and over the *V* of the
sweater to the applause of Mr. Rosini's quiet smile. An hour later,
however, I felt anything but sensual. I was holed up by myself in
the hot copy room with a stack of reports waiting to be multiplied,
tired and sweaty from the stale, too-warm exhalations of all the
office machines. I tossed off my black blazer, but sweat still beaded
up in my cleavage. I grabbed a tissue and dabbed at it while I
watched the machine work, reaching far between my D-cups so
that I'd feel halfway dry again. My breasts jiggled—it's kind of
unavoidable when you're my size—and my nipples responded to

the motion by making themselves very obvious through my sweater. Suddenly I wanted to tease them with my fingertips. The thought of Mr. Rosini's soft voice and the scent of strong coffee began to make me feel a bit fluttery between my legs. That custard of his, I mused to myself, must be the essence of the gods.

"Hey, Julie, could you...." Luke, a new intern, walked into the copy room. He saw me, then stopped as if he'd just walked into a wall. In my attempts to dehumidify the undersides of my breasts, a good two-thirds of one nipple had begun to peek over the neckline of my sweater, and the hemline had ridden up, exposing an inch or three of my well-padded middle. I'd been too distracted to notice.

"Um...I..." Luke stammered, then frowned and looked down at the papers he held. "I need ten of these." He set them on a counter, then wheeled around and left. I saw his eyes roll upward and the grimace on his lips as he walked out the door.

"Oh, shit," I said to no one in particular, and straightened my clothes again.

Several days later, on a cold rainy morning that brought in droves of people seeking hot coffee and warm muffins, I wound up at Rosini's Bakery again. Ed Rosini was behind the counter, doling out muffins, boxing up doughnuts, and talking with the customers. I sat at my usual table, off to the side, and watched the rain fall from the steely sky. I was preparing myself for a day of raised eyebrows and disapproving looks at work, having decided to wear a navy blue broomstick skirt that floated from my hips in a gauzy cloud and a scarlet silk peasant blouse, the limits of whose ruffled neckline were being pushed by a pushup bra. Having fantastic cleavage makes a fine antidote to depressing weather.

"Hello, my Polish flower," Mr. Rosini stood beside me with a tray. Mr. Rosini never calls me by name, though he knows it. He only calls me "my Polish flower" or sometimes "my dear." On the tray was a steaming cup of coffee, a tiny pitcher of cream, and a small dish of sugar. He placed them on my table.

"Mr. Rosini, I could have gotten that at the counter," I said, but I was grateful for the service.

"No, no," he said. "Too many people. You'd stand at the counter forever." He smiled as I poured cream into the coffee, stirring it from dark brown to light tan. "My dear," Mr. Rosini continued in a low voice, "you look lovely as ever."

"Thank you, Mr. Rosini." I smiled up at him with a sideways glance and took a deep breath, my cantilevered cleavage rising and falling in time. I heard a soft intake of breath from Mr. Rosini.

"Now," he bowed slightly forward, his hands folded, "What shall we try today?" I wondered what Mr. Rosini would have done the other day in the copy room had he been the intern who'd walked in? I wondered if he would have shut the door, locked us in, taken my hands in his, and kissed them before running a finger along my errant nipple. Would he have kissed the cleft between my breasts and licked the sweat away?

I leaned forward a bit, giving Mr. Rosini a better view as I craned my neck to survey the glass case at the back of the store where he and his son had lovingly laid out the fruits of their labors. Cream horns, muffins, fruit tarts, and pies nestled together in rows. An angelic tiramisu sat on a glass cake plate. I'd been the fortunate eater of Mr. Rosini's tiramisu on a number of occasions and can confidently say that I have known tiramisu heaven. The thought of his artistry melting in my mouth made my mouth water, and, what was more, that fluttery feeling between my legs flashed to life again.

"Ah, Mr. Rosini, I can't decide. You pick for me," I sighed. He nodded solemnly and walked away. I turned back to view the narrow, rain-slicked streets where the cars hurtled past one another, spaces the width of a sheet of paper between them. The door opened as a cluster of customers trudged into the shop, and a blast of cold air hit me. I grinned at the sensation of my nipples' response to the cold air, and smiled with satisfaction at the timing.

"Here you are, my dear." Mr. Rosini placed a white plate on the table. On it sat a cream horn nestled on a red paper doily, powdered sugar dusted over the pastry and the red paper below. "I made these this morning. The shell is as delicate as I've ever made."

Mr. Rosini pulled up a chair and sat next to me. I looked at the pastry for a moment, then scooped a bit of cream from the end with my finger, sucking it off with relish. Mr. Rosini waited patiently while I picked up the cream horn, sniffed its buttery aroma, then took the first bite. As was usual with most of Mr. Rosini's filled pastries, it was overstuffed, and when I bit down much of the cream spurted out the sides, decorating the corners of my mouth. I desperately licked my lips in an effort to catch it, but inevitably some of it made its way onto my cheek and chin.

"There's just no dainty way to eat a cream horn," Mr. Rosini apologized, cradling my chin in his fingertips and dabbing at the cream on my face with a paper napkin. My heartbeat quickened. I sighed, chewing, feeling my heavy breasts strain against the blouse as the pastry dissolved like snowflakes in my mouth, cream tickling my tongue with its airy sweetness and the faintest hint of amaretto.

"Now tell me: How do you like it, my dear?" Mr. Rosini whispered above the din of the bustling customers, tense as he waited for my answer.

Tears prickled my eyelids at his expectant, hopeful schoolboy's expression. I swallowed and steadied my voice. "Mr. Rosini, it's very lovely," I said, immediately feeling stupid for using such a common phrase to describe something akin to Venus's birth on the oyster shell. He wiped the corners of my eyes with a paper napkin, smiled, and covered my hands with his. I sniffled and clasped his soft, wrinkled hands.

"Hey, Dad!" his son barked from behind the counter. Mr. Rosini looked up and nodded at Ed, standing sentry as the customers lined up three deep.

I finished my pastry alone and drank the rest of my coffee as the rain outside let up. When I was done, Mr. Rosini stacked my coffee cup on my empty plate, and refused to let me pay, shaking his head at me as I took out my wallet and waving my money away. He picked up my raincoat, gave it a soft shake, and helped me into it. I carefully slipped my arms through the sleeves, a shiver racing down my spine when he adjusted the collar and his fingertips brushed my neck. And then I left Rosini's Bakery and headed for work.

By midafternoon I was back at Rosini's. My supervisor at the law firm had told me—in a strained voice, barely able to look me in the eye—to take the rest of the day off. She wouldn't say so, but I knew it was because of the blouse. They didn't like it and wouldn't tolerate it, and I hadn't brought a severe black jacket to go over it, either. Not very professional, I know. In my office, even the broomstick skirt was pushing the envelope.

By the time I got to Rosini's, it was closed. I knew it would be, but I stood outside in the doorway alcove, the rain pouring, my feet sopping wet. The venetian blinds in the front window were drawn and shut, but suddenly there was a rattling and the door opened. Mr. Rosini stood there, welcoming me with an understanding smile.

"I knew you'd be back," he softly said as he let me into the store. I stood there, my rain coat dripping water on the floor, my face and hair damp. "Where's your umbrella?"

"I left it in the car," I replied. The lights were off in the front room of the bakery, and the light-green walls looked gray and cold, but I could see white light emanating from the kitchen and heard the sound of a violin singing sweetly from a radio. Mr. Rosini took my hand and led me back to the big kitchen, spacious, white, and bright, smelling of sugar and dough. He pulled out a chair from a table and gestured to me to sit down.

"Coffee?" he asked, as if he needed to.

"Yes, thank you, Mr. Rosini," I replied, suddenly feeling weary. He filled a white cup with fresh coffee, bringing cream and sugar along with it. "You've been closed for an hour, " I commented when he placed these things before me.

"So I have," he replied without missing a beat, his voice and manner polite and quiet as usual.

"And where is your son?" I asked, pouring cream in the coffee until it turned pale brown.

"I sent him on a road trip. To see our accountant," he replied, smiling at me. I nodded and stirred sugar into my coffee. The violin music strained high and low. The coffee warmed my hands as we smiled at one another and Mr. Rosini sat back in his chair. Then, suddenly, he slipped to the floor, kneeling at my feet.

He slipped off my shoes, tsk-tsking as he did so. "These are fine shoes and they're all wet. Your stockings," he squeezed my feet, "they're soaking, too. We should remove these as well. We can't have you in wet clothes." His long-fingered hands traveled up my legs, over thick ankles and calves, up to my meaty thighs and my round tummy. I inhaled as his deft fingers hooked inside the waistband of my pantyhose and tugged, gripping the edges of my chair with my hands and lifting my hips. The hose slid down, and Mr. Rosini slipped his hands underneath me to slide them out from underneath my bottom, his hands squeezing and pushing against my full cheeks. I watched through half-closed eyes as he slid the hose—Queen size, "Barely Nude"—over my thighs, pushing my skirt up to my hips, exposing the crotch of my red silky briefs. Finally he pulled them past knees, ankles, and toes, and then they were gone, and Mr. Rosini was carefully pulling my skirt back down to my calves.

Mr. Rosini shook the hose and hung them over the back of a chair, the thin fabric still curving where my legs had stretched a limp question mark into them. He placed my shoes by a heating vent, then he sat back down at the table. He rested his arms on the table, and we stared at one another for a moment.

"I have something I've been working on. It's on the stove. Would you like to try it?" He nodded toward the stove. I nodded and smiled, shifting my weight from one ass cheek to the next, remembering Mr. Rosini's hands there, kneading and poking. Mr. Rosini brought a pan to the table. It was filled with a pale yellow custard, and the tangy scent of lemon tickled my nostrils.

"Lemon custard. Slowly cooked, not mercilessly boiled. Gently simmered and stirred and stirred until, in its own fine time, it turns into silk." He stirred the custard and ladled out a spoonful, then turned the spoon upside down, letting the custard fell back into the pan with a soft, lazy plop. "Would you like a taste, my dear?"

"Yes," I whispered.

Mr. Rosini gathered up a spoonful and put it to my lips. "Blow on it," he ordered, and I did, then opened my mouth. Mr. Rosini slid the spoon in. I closed my eyes and moaned as the silky custard bathed the insides of my mouth. I swirled my tongue against the lemony thick sweetness, then swallowed. When I opened my eyes, Mr. Rosini's face was close to mine. "You like it?" he asked in a hoarse voice.

"Oh, yes, I do," I whispered. He cupped my chin with his fingers, then kissed me. I expected seventy-year-old lips to be colder, thinner, but his were warm and firm. He stroked my lips with them, caressing my cheeks with his fingers, then pulled away and held my face in his hands.

"Why do you let them hurt you so?" I placed my hands on his and closed my eyes, the vision of Luke the intern and my dour supervisor in her brown suit glaring at me from some kind of made-up judges' bench.

"I don't know, actually," I replied.

"Look at me," he implored. I did. "Here, you are in your own realm. Here, you reign, you are a woman, a Madonna," he said, kissing my hands, then looked up at me. "You think I'm a foolish old man. But believe me, I'm not. I've seen more of life than you."

Actually, I didn't think him a foolish old man at all, but before I could refute his statement, he drew me into his arms and kissed me long and hard. His torso, warm and wiry, pressed against my round softness. I wriggled my chest against him, hoping he would caress my breasts. When he pulled away and still didn't caress me, I unbuttoned my blouse and placed his hands on my breasts. He stroked me through the silken cups of my bra, then caressed the crested tops. I reached into my bra cups and lifted each breast from its cradle, letting them hang. Then Mr. Rosini's hands kneaded and pinched, and he bent his head and suckled one of my dark brown nipples. I moaned as the violin music from the radio gently filtered through the room. I cupped my breasts and offered them to him as he kissed and licked.

Oh, he was right. I am Madonna, I am alive. I feel life rush through my veins, I thought. I cradled Mr. Rosini's head to my breasts as he suckled, his white hair soft in my fingers as I stroked it and cooed. The cold Pittsburgh rain pounded against the shop. I spread my legs and pushed at Mr. Rosini's shoulders, and again he knelt before me.

"My dear," he said as he pushed up my skirt, "I am sick with jealousy when I see the young men look at you." He bent his head and kissed the inside of my thigh. Heat quivered from that spot to my labia, then to my clit.

"They're not looking at me," I politely argued as I spread my legs wide for him. His hands caressed my hips and before I knew it, my red panties were off.

"No?" he asked, then kissed my mound. "You think not?" his voice hissed, then he mouthed my entire vulva. I wriggled and whimpered, spreading my labia wide. "You think they don't want to know what I have now? You think they don't want to know your scent? To see this flesh weep and spread for them? No?"

I shook my head. He gripped either side of my thighs and plunged his tongue into my folds. I cried out with the jolt that ran through my body. His tongue licked one side of my pussy from bottom to top, pausing to flick my clit, then licked down the other side, ending where my juices flowed. He pulled away and looked at me with his big brown eyes, his forehead creased. "Yes, oh yes, they do! Oh, believe me, my flower, I understand. I'm a man. I have desires, I have a heart, I have a soul. Young man—old man. It doesn't matter. When we see a beautiful woman who enjoys the simple pleasures of the morning, who stirs her coffee as though she has all the time in the world, we want her."

"Mmm," I whimpered, stroking my wet labia. I was hungry and needed to be filled.

"Tell me you haven't noticed the men here who look at you. They walk out of here, reaching into their coat pocket for car keys, and when they see you, their hands falter and they smile at you. Tell me you haven't seen this." He squeezed my thighs hard. Of course, here in my old neighborhood, the old-worldy neighborhood, I'd seen their admiring looks. I felt flushed and gripped his hands to stop.

"Yes, I've seen it," I admitted.

"Mmm-hmm," he replied, grim but satisfied. "Jealous, my flower. I am a jealous man." And he rested his cheek against my leg with a sigh.

"But you need not be," I said, pushing his head off my leg and thrusting my hips to his face. He plunged his tongue into me. I squeezed his face with my thick thighs and rubbed my feet on his back. He probed and flicked his tongue until I climaxed, not once, but twice.

As I had been wrong about his lips, I was also wrong about Mr. Rosini's cock. When he stood over me, I could see the bulge under his zipper. I let him fumble with the zipper, figuring I would take even longer with my trembling hands, but I did pull his cock out of his briefs, clasping it in my warm hand, feeling the veins of his shaft as I stroked and squeezed.

"Ah, my dear, not here," he said, cupping my face and looking down at me. "I need to take you somewhere...better," he sighed.

"No," I said. "Here. Please, now."

I stroked him again and he winced. The corners of his mouth hitched up in a smile. "It is very difficult to say no to you."

He stroked my hair, then suddenly pulled on the bun and my hair fell loose around my face. "Ah, such an angel," he sighed, teasing the bouncy strands. I rose from the chair and hoisted myself onto the table. I yanked my skirt up to my waist and petted my mound. "Ah, God," Mr. Rosini ran his hands down his face as he looked at me. I wet my fingers with my own juices, then licked my fingers. I gazed into his eyes, then glanced down at his bobbing cock.

He sighed again. "I assume you don't want babies?"

"Someday," I smiled.

He looked sternly at me. "I mean right now."

"No, not right now," I replied.

Mr. Rosini stared at me a moment, the palms of his hands on his face. Then a thought seemed to hit him. "Just a moment, my dear." He went to a small office off the kitchen. I could not see him, but heard him opening drawers and shuffling papers.

After a while he walked back into the kitchen with a wrapped condom, holding it up with a wry smile. "Since my son's divorce...he, ah, you know...is quite popular with the ladies, you see." I understood. He shook his head, looking sheepish. "I don't even know how to use this." I held out my hand and he gave the package to me. I carefully opened it, then took out the condom, then drew his cock out of his pants again.

I sensed his embarrassment, so I held his cock in my hand and kissed him, pumping him gently until he was very firm. I placed the condom on the tip of his cock, a little sorry to have to cover the clear drops that had dripped out, then unrolled it to his base. "All done," I said, patting his tummy with a smile.

He frowned. "How can a man pleasure a woman this way?" I laughed and placed his hands on my breasts. He laughed too, after a moment, and bent down to kiss me. I leaned back on the table and guided Mr. Rosini's cock to my vulva. I rubbed it up and down my labia, as he had done with his tongue, teasing my clit with the tip, then placed him at my opening. I was swollen and dripping wet, and with one decisive push, Mr. Rosini was inside me. I gasped at the sudden intrusion but soon urged him to stroke inside me, wrapping my legs around his waist.

Mr. Rosini was stronger than I thought, clasping handfuls of flesh on my hips, thrusting. I squeezed him with my thighs, his hips lost in my flesh. I had to lie back on the table to take him deeper, unwrapped my legs from his waist, and pulled them back, spreading wide for him. He touched me deep. His movements were slow and methodical, like stirring and simmering. Gentle, patient stirring, waiting and waiting and watching and finally...

"Oh, please!" I gasped, bucking my hips for more. And he obliged with deep, hard thrusts, and in my own good time I climaxed. "Oh, God, yes," I groaned, clasping his hands at my hips.

"God, indeed," he said, his voice tight. I kept bucking and

moaning, not to achieve another orgasm, but because that one was so long and powerful. I finally opened my eyes and realized Mr. Rosini had not climaxed. His mouth was taut and his eyes narrow.

"What is it?" I whispered, reaching for him. "Is it the condom?" He drew in a deep breath and held still.

"No, no...it's not that. I...ah...my dear, " he sighed and closed his eyes. He carefully pulled himself out of me. "Stand up," he whispered. I looked at him for a moment, then took the hand he offered.

"Turn around." He turned me to face the table and I leaned into it as he lifted my skirt and pressed his body against mine. His hands cupped my full ass cheeks and his cock poked insistently. I understood and pressed my ass into him. We ground our bodies together for a moment, but when I heard him breathe sharp and hard, I lay myself flat on the table top, feet wide apart on the floor, listening to his deep, guttural noises. His hands were on my ass, pushing and pulling. Up and out he kneaded my flesh, his fingers squeezing and pulling.

Blessed is the dough that is greeted by Mr. Rosini's hands each morning, I thought, smiling, and resting my head on my arms as he worked me, gently slapping and patting, then kneading again. "I must have you now," he whispered, then placed the tip of his cock at the entrance of my pussy. I breathed deep to accept him and we both grunted when he slid into me.

I knew I wouldn't climax again, but Mr. Rosini was enthralled, and that alone was enough pleasure for me. He glided inside me, moaning with each push. He buried himself deeper and deeper, touching that lovely spot so deep inside me, and although I didn't need that spot scratched again, it was good to feel it bloom against Mr. Rosini's thrusts.

"Ah, my flower, my flower," he moaned at last, out of breath, somewhere between sobbing and laughing. He leaned on me, his face buried in my hair, his hands clasping mine. I drank in the scent of his sweat and body. He placed soft kisses on the side of my neck. After a while, we stood up. He wet a clean dish cloth with hot water at the sink and offered it to me. I used it to dab at my vulva and held it there for a moment to soothe the well-worked folds as Mr. Rosini put himself back together.

We were silent as he helped me do the same. My pantyhose were dry, but my shoes were not. "We'll let them dry a bit longer," Mr. Rosini said.

As he buttoned my blouse, he shook his head. "A real gentleman would have found a more suitable place."

I took his hands in mine and kissed them. "But here, in your kitchen, I am in my realm," I replied. "You said so."

He smiled from ear to ear, reaching up to tuck a wayward curl behind my ear, both of us giggling softly at the sound of a car door slamming outside in the alley—Mr. Rosini's son, returning from his errand.

"Hey, Dad," Ed called as he banged through the doorway, "the accountant said there wasn't a tax problem at all, he has no idea what you were going on about...."

Ed's voice stopped suddenly as he saw me there, standing in his father's kitchen. "Hey there, Julie," he said, his eyes widening with pleased surprise, "Didn't expect to see you again today. You look amazing in that outfit, though—didn't get a chance to tell you this morning. Hope you didn't get too wet out there! The old man been taking good care of you?"

"Yes, of course he has," I replied, with a fond glance at Mr. Rosini.

Ed left to hang up his sodden trenchcoat. Mr. Rosini leaned in, his lips grazing my ear lightly, his voice gently proud and amused. "You see, my Polish flower? I was right."

CLEAVAGE

Diana Lee

The lights were intentionally low at the dungeon, with some spotlights around the play areas so that those who enjoyed watching could do so without intruding. Gwen watched now as a woman was bound to a St. Andrew's Cross: a large wooden *X* that was bolted to the dungeon wall, picked out by a fierce white pin spot. The bottom was dressed only in a thong, and Gwen shivered in sympathy as a cold metal chain was wound around the woman's waist and locked in place. As the dominant moved up behind the bound woman and began caressing her exposed ass cheeks, Gwen's breathing became more rapid. The anticipation of the beating-to-come was something that Gwen could completely identify with. As the woman top's resounding slap brought a pink flush to the bottom's ass, Gwen felt someone move behind her, and she half turned to see who had come up to stand looking over her shoulder.

The face was familiar, a very studly butch she had admired from afar but whom she'd never actually met. There was a rapt look on the other woman's face, but Gwen realized she wasn't watching the spanking that was unfolding in front of them. The butch's eyes were firmly fixed on Gwen's cleavage.

It had taken Gwen almost an hour of experimenting to get the effect she'd wanted. She had to take the bodice in by two inches to get the tight fit around her midriff that would support her breasts. The cut of the bodice was just a little too high, and she'd been disappointed that it merely pressed her breasts flat when she first put it on. Well, not flat—they could never really be flat. Finally, she had come upon the solution of unlacing the top two holes and letting the front of the bodice gape open. That way, the stiff leather lifted and cradled her breasts at the same time, creating the perfect setting for her more-than-generous cleavage. It was an effect worth the small amount of discomfort the tight leather caused.

The cleft between the two soft mounds of Gwen's breasts was deeply shadowed and ran in a gentle curve for several inches: a deep ravine hiding a multitude of mysteries. The breasts themselves were past being firm and round, but ran in soft ovals that were restrained by a cradle of black leather. It was the kind of cleavage in which a woman could bury both her hands; the kind of cleavage a woman could cradle her head on, dreaming of floating on clouds of opulent flesh.

The scene ended with a flurry of blows, the bottom writhing and screaming. Then the top was there, cradling the woman against her, whispering endearments. Gwen turned away. It never embarrassed her to watch a scene, but looking at the two women sharing the intimacy of the aftercare made Gwen feel like a voyeur. Even watching the sex that sometimes became part of a scene did not feel as much of an intrusion as watching this kind of tenderness. Gwen turned her wheelchair carefully, mindful of the toes that she might run over as she maneuvered. The butch who'd been watching her breasts was still there, so Gwen turned to face her, a complacent smile on her face.

"Ummm, nice tattoo," the butch offered, slightly embarrassed to be caught staring so openly. Gwen's smiled deepened both at the compliment and at the thought that butches really were so shy.

"Thank you. My name is Gwen. I've seen you at a couple of play parties, but I don't think we've ever met before."

"No, we haven't, and that has definitely been my loss," the butch answered gallantly. "My name is Val." She put her hand out, and Gwen took it, a bit confused. Its seemed strange to shake hands in such a setting, but Val surprised her again, bowing and lifting Gwen's hand to her lips.

Gwen's smile grew till two dimples appeared in her plump cheeks. "It is a pleasure, indeed, to meet you, Sir Val."

"May I get you a drink?" Val offered, and Gwen asked for a seltzer. Gwen watched Val move away through the crowd. She admired the butch woman's blue-jeaned legs and tight ass, but what had caught her eye at previous play parties had been the other woman's style. Val was not tall, but she projected presence. She wore a black, buccaneer-style shirt with flared sleeves gathered into tight cuffs. The way she wore the shirt was graceful without being the least bit feminine. Val's straight black hair was closely cropped, and Gwen admired the way the light caught the sprinkling of white hairs scattered in the black. The butch's face was strong but showed laugh lines around the eyes and mouth.

She wasn't outstandingly handsome, though she had a comfortable face with solid, dark brows and gray eyes. Her lips were a little too thin, her nose a little bent, adding character rather than prettiness.

Gwen had watched Val at play before, and had liked what she had seen. It had been a scene involving a young butch boi creature who seemed to be new to the leather scene. Gwen had admired the way Val had stroked the boi and reassured her continually as she had first spanked and flogged, and then wielded a heavy leather paddle. She'd worked slowly, backing off the minute the boi showed any real discomfort, allowing the inexperienced bottom the time to process the pain at her own pace. Gwen had liked Val's patience and tenderness. It bespoke a top who appreciated the gift of submission, who offered as much respect to her bottoms as she expected as a top. Gwen had particularly loved the way Val had alternated her increasingly hard blows with soft caresses. For a big bad butch top, Val showed wonderful sensitivity and care.

Val walked back toward Gwen carrying two drinks, a heavy, black leather toy bag slung over her shoulder. Gwen's heart quickened, anticipating being asked, afraid of *not* being asked.

Val gave Gwen her drink and set the heavy bag down next to Gwen's chair. Her eyes held Gwen's a moment, assessing, and then she let her gaze drift down to Gwen's cleavage again. "May I?"

Gwen nodded, and Val lifted the stiff leather of the bodice away from Gwen's left breast, completely exposing her tattoo. Val traced the petals of the deep pink orchid with her finger tips, the gentle touch making Gwen draw her breath in sharply. Val circled the lower petal that lay open and exposed, her gesture making the flower's resemblance to labia that much more obvious. She slid her finger along Gwen's soft, warm flesh, straight into the center of the orchid where it pulsed with a deeper pink.

"I think you know what I want," Val said, holding Gwen's gaze again.

Negotiations took no time at all. Gwen's eyes had strayed

to Val's crotch earlier in the evening, and she had noted that the butch was packing. Somehow, as they had talked about the coming scene, it seemed to Gwen that the bulge in Val's jeans had grown. It was a physical impossibility, of course, but, Gwen reminded herself, perceptions could change with mood. A safe-word was agreed on, and Val shouldered her toy bag again.

Val moved behind Gwen's chair and wheeled her over to a low platform. Gwen's heart was racing in anticipation, but she took deep, even breaths, centering herself. "How do you want me?" Gwen asked simply as they reached the platform.

"Take everything off but the vest. I want to see you."

Gwen stood a little shakily and pulled her velvet skirt up over her head. Under the skirt she wore a pair of black bicycle shorts that showed the outlines of her flesh. Feeling Val staring at her, she shimmed her hips just a little before pulling the shorts down so that she was naked below the waist.

Gwen looked at Val, and there was nothing submissive in the challenge in her gaze. Val stared back, clearly enjoying the view. As their eyes met, Val's grin broadened. Val held Gwen's eyes for a long moment, testing her will, then she chuckled deep in her throat and turned to open her toy bag. She wouldn't need very much from it tonight, but some other night, she thought to herself as she rummaged, she would possess that lovely ass. Val licked her lips, thinking of the enormous white canvas Gwen's ass would offer, imagining the marks she could leave on all that soft flesh. Another time.

Gwen watched Val turn away, and she wondered just what the wicked gleam in the butch's eyes might portend. As she took the two steps to the platform, her breath quickened with antici-pation. Her heart started beating faster as she sat facing Val. Whatever evil thoughts Val was having, Gwen was more than ready to play the victim to them.

Val folded the wheelchair and moved it out of the way. It was an act more meaningful than perhaps she realized, for now Gwen could not move from where she sat. Gwen took a deep breath, sinking deeper into sub space. Her perceptions contracted around herself and Val, her senses becoming more and more heightened. Sub space was a place of complete trust, the giving over of power, a feeling of freedom like pumping higher and higher on a swing until the ground was far away, then pushing off into space secure in the knowledge that Val would be there to catch her. Gwen did not need bondage to feel the pleasurable helplessness of being in someone else's power. She couldn't escape now. Not that she really wanted to. That was the paradox and joy of submission for Gwen: the knowledge that, having made the choice to give over her power, she was both amazingly helpless and incredibly free.

Val stepped up in front of Gwen, and Gwen's face was now level with Val's belt. She bent her head and rubbed her cheek against the bulge in Val's jeans. The butch laughed, tangling her fingers in Gwen's long hair and pulling her head back.

"Eager for it, aren't you, slut?" Val asked softly.

"Yes, Mas..." Gwen began, less than meek until she realized she might be overstepping her bounds.

Val jerked her head back farther and kissed her roughly. "You will have to earn the right to call me Master. 'Sir' will do for now."

"Yes, Sir."

Val felt a frisson of pleasure at being addressed as "Sir." It was as if her head expanded, the first seductive flare of power flickering to life in her consciousness. It was not just the word, of course, but the need behind it, the subtle plea in Gwen's tone, that fired Val's desire to both hurt and pleasure this woman.

Val ran her lips along Gwen's exposed throat. She could feel Gwen's pulse pounding against her lips, and she smiled as she licked the vulnerable pulse point. Later she would give this woman a mark to remember her by. Now she licked her way down to that lovely cleavage, feeling the other woman shudder and moan with pleasure.

Val stepped back to look at her victim: Gwen sat wearing only the black leather bodice, held together over her midriff by purple suede laces, the points of the bodice lying against Gwen's soft belly. Val traced the bottom of the two points, just barely caressing tender belly skin. She pressed her palm against it and wondered what it would feel like to lie on top of someone so soft. There were no awkwardly jutting bones in this woman, Val thought as she smiled. She ran her palms down to the bottom of the softly falling belly, lifting the heavy fold to expose Gwen's mons. Val grinned toothily, visibly enjoying the adventure of having to hunt for Gwen's sex.

Val nudged Gwen's legs apart with her knee, but it wasn't enough. She pushed Gwen's legs wide open, spreading her with two hands and a delicious, leering look. Now, finally, she could see the deeper pink flesh peeking out between the mounds of Gwen's thighs. She smiled as she ran her fingers over Gwen's lips, her grin deepening as she felt the wetness. Gwen moaned loudly and thrust her hips forward.

"Later, slut." Val commanded. "That's another thing you will have to earn."

"Yes, Sir," Gwen said, nodding. She was deep in sub space already, aware of the other women in the room, but only as shadows caught in her peripheral vision. Her world consisted only of sensation. Her rational mind told her that this was a stranger before her, and that she needed to be careful, but there was nothing very rational left in her.

Val examined Gwen's face. The shape was an oval, made longer by the soft double chin. Gwen had lovely dark eyes, the brown of them soft and warm and shadowed by strong brows that had a soft, natural curve. Her mouth was a perfect cupid's bow, and Val could not resist kissing the soft lips once more. They parted, inviting her in, and Val, being the gentleperson she was, accepted the invitation, invading with her tongue.

Val slipped her hands into the bodice, finally giving in to her desire to crush those lovely breasts. She pushed them together and squeezed until Gwen squealed, still holding her mouth prisoner. Val's fingers hunted, diving deep to find the nipples. They were half hardened, and she trapped them both between her fingers, pulling up until they were freed from the leather. She pulled back a bit now, looking at how Gwen's breasts lay on top of the leather bodice. They pulled it down some, but the leather still kept the two breasts nestled together. That was important. Val caressed over the tops, and then her fingers delved deep into the soft-walled valley. It was her turn to moan, but she bit the sound back. A butch top just didn't let on how very aroused she was.

Gwen's eyes were closed, lost in the pleasure of Val's caresses, until Val stroked her cheek to get her attention. Gwen looked into Val's eyes, seeing the desire within them.

"Are you ready?" Val asked.

"Yes, Sir." The words were almost soundless.

Val picked up the nipple clamps she had taken out of her bag. They were shiny silver with complex spring hinges between handles joined by a short chain. When the chain was pulled, the clamps would tighten. Val bent and kissed Gwen's right nipple. She sucked it into her mouth, feeling it harden even more. Her tongue played with the hard ridges that formed around the edge until she heard Gwen moaning again. Then she pulled back and took the nipple firmly between her thumb and forefinger, stretching it out, holding Gwen's eyes with her own as she let the clamp close around the tender nipple.

Gwen hissed as the clamp bit, taking several deep breaths before she could process the pain. Then she nodded.

She was ready.

Val weighed the other breast in her hand. Her thumb caressed the nipple while she squeezed the soft flesh. It overflowed her hand, and she loved the way her fingers sank deep into the flesh of it, wishing that she had longer nails so that they could add a soft counterpoint of pain. Gwen was leaning back a bit now, her arms supporting her as she arched her breasts out toward Val. Val took the nipple between her fingers and pulled it out, closing the second clamp around the nipple. Then she pulled sharply on the chain, and the clamps tightened.

Gwen screamed softly. It took her long moments to control her breathing again as the fiery pain emanated up from her nipples along her breasts. The clamps had been made for a much smaller person, and so the chain was stretched tight across her torso, holding her nipples a good four inches closer than they normally lay, and each breath added another jagged shock of pain.

Val was smiling as she watched Gwen process the pain. Her hand had unconsciously gone to her own crotch, and she was stroking the bulge in her jeans as she watched Gwen assimilate the sensation and let it flow through her. When Gwen looked up at her, Val nodded her head in admiration. She caressed Gwen's cheek and kissed her again, this time gently.

Val cupped Gwen's breasts and squeezed. She heard and felt Gwen scream against her lips, adding another layer to the spiral of pleasure that twined between the two women. Val stepped back again, and reached down to unzip her jeans.

It was time.

Gwen watched as Val freed the cock from her boxers and brought it out. Gwen hesitantly reached out to touch it, and Val nodded her permission. Gwen stroked along the shaft, cradling the cock in both hands. Her thumbs caressed the head much as Val's fingers had caressed Gwen's nipples. She bent her head and took the head in her mouth, moaning as she ran her tongue over the smooth surface. Val's hips thrust, and Gwen opened her mouth to take the cock deeper, sucking hard enough for Val to feel the base of the cock moving against her. Gwen moaned in pleasure, enjoying the feel of Val's cock filling her mouth. She looked up through her lashes at the butch, longing to see the other woman as lost in pleasure as Gwen herself was.

Val smiled at Gwen's obvious enjoyment, but pulled out of her mouth. There was a subtle struggle for power as Val took firm control of her own sexual needs. Gwen was having a greater effect on her than Val had anticipated, and Val could see that knowledge in Gwen's eyes. Val decided she would allow her this small victory, but there would be a price to pay. Of *course* there would be a price, the top chuckled to herself.

Val squeezed a generous bit of lube on her cock and rubbed it along the length of it. She pushed Gwen back on the platform and threaded her cock under the chain holding the nipple clamps, pushing up between Gwen's breasts. The chain pulled the clamps tighter as it strained around Val's cock, and Gwen screamed again, then began to sink into the sensations as Val began thrusting up between her breasts.

Val marveled that Gwen's breasts completely swallowed her cock. She could feel the friction as she pulled out and the pressure as she thrust back in. Only the very tip of the head peeked out between Gwen's breasts, and Val stood watching as she thrust in and out for a while, enjoying the view of her shaft sinking into that lovely, deep cleavage.

Suddenly she straddled Gwen, pushing her farther back against the platform. Now Val's thrusts were harder, more urgent. Her body slammed into the soft belly beneath her, and she smiled in pure pleasure. Gwen's breasts rode up against the zipper of Val's jeans, and Val could feel their softness as she rammed the cock deep into Gwen's cleavage as Gwen writhed beneath her. Each thrust pulled the chain between the nipple clamps, tightening them in subtle increments.

Gwen was caught in the spiral between pain and pleasure. The sensation of Val's smooth cock between her breasts was incredibly sensuous, and the pain, rather than distracting her, only added to Gwen's arousal. She rocked her breasts up to meet Val's thrusts, immersed in the contrast of sensations. She heard Val's breathing become more ragged, felt her body shuddering, and smelled her juices as Val collapsed on top of her.

Val braced herself on her arms, not wanting to let her full weight fall on Gwen's face. It took a long, dizzying moment for her to catch her breath, and still the softly heaving breasts beneath her were sending shocks of sensation through her cock and into her cunt. For once, she wished that her butch pride would allow her to be demonstrative of her own needs, because she wanted to crush her wet cunt against one of those soft breasts so badly she could taste it, so badly she could feel it in her clit. Perhaps another time when things were more private she would do just that, she thought, as she pulled back slowly, mindful of the chain.

Val stood up and tucked the cock back into her boxers. She looked around surreptitiously as she zipped her jeans up again. She didn't normally display this much of herself at a play party. Then she sat next to Gwen and helped her sit up. The clamps had been on too long, and they both knew it. Val cradled Gwen's head against her shoulder and whispered her thanks in her ear, kissing her softly and holding her as she caught her breath.

"I need to take the clamps off," Val said softly. "It'll hurt like hell."

Gwen shuddered. "I know." She took several deep breaths to center herself, and then nodded her readiness. Val snatched off the first clamp, and Gwen muffled a scream against the butch's shoulder. For long moments, all Gwen was aware of was the pounding in her breast. Val held her hand over the sore nipple until the pounding diminished to a bearable level, then she removed the second clamp. This time, Gwen's scream escaped, and several people looked over, nodding knowingly. Val stroked Gwen's hair until she had assimilated the pain, soothing her, calming her.

"Perhaps I should get a longer chain put on these," Val said thoughtfully as she held the clamps up in demonstration, tacitly asking for an encore.

Gwen smiled, not too shy to catch Val's eye as the other woman's gaze drifted across her cleavage again. "No," she replied, accepting as subtly as Val had offered. "Leave them the way they are."

GODDESS
WORSHIP

Reyna D. Tutto

I wasn't the only person on campus who had a crush on Wyoming Smith, just the one lucky enough to be asked to house-sit for him when both he and his lover had to be out of town. Being a graduate student doesn't have many perks, but house-sitting for the hottest prof on campus is one of them. Eyebrows rose all over the Archaeology department the afternoon Wyo made it public that I'd be the designated mail drop for those two weeks, and that anything anyone needed to drop off for him, they could just hand to me. It wasn't that I wasn't trustworthy, and it wasn't as if I wasn't one of the senior grad students in the department, but I wasn't one of the usual suspects. You see, Wyoming's preferences were well known, and, well, I'm not a boy.

Not that it mattered to me whether I was his type—not really. I had it bad for Dr. Smith, and it wasn't just the size of his prodigious intellect that made me weak in the knees. It was the size of everything, from the thousand-watt smile and thick, well-kept beard to the treetrunk thighs that filled out the legs of his battered jeans like a strong wind bellying out a mainsail. It was the way he walked, graceful like the athlete he was, the roll of his sexy, powerful stride magnified enormously by his size and the weight he put behind his movements. Dr. Wyoming Smith was four hundred pounds of tall, strong, unapologetic male animal, and he was, very simply, hot as hell.

I'd been crushed out on him for at least a year, oblivious to pretty much anyone else. I didn't give a damn that some of my women friends didn't get it. They'd say things like "Well, if he were thinner I'd see your point. He'd be cute if he'd just lose some weight." As far as I was concerned, Wyo Smith didn't need to lose an ounce, and he wasn't "cute." He was goddamned magnificent, and I didn't give a damn if there wasn't another woman on campus who agreed. I didn't give a damn that he was gay, either—or that half the men I knew dreamed longingly of what it would be like to be held against that enormous furry chest, because I did too.

I tried so hard to be good when I house-sat, honestly I did. I didn't snoop, I didn't even go up the stairs to the second floor of the house Wyo shared with his architect lover, Turner. Downstairs, at least, the house felt comfortably jumbled, the personalities of two very different men mingling in the downstairs rooms, Italian modern furniture sitting cheek by jowl with enormous, primitive wooden fetishes studded with thousands of nails, New Guinean penis gourds, and a large Andean feather headdress. Tibetan blankets hung over the back of the sleek leather sofa, and innumerable exotic trinkets sat on the bookshelves and next to piles of design magazines on the coffee table. It wasn't hard to imagine the two men sitting there, even in their absence.

It was a good place, comfortable and warm, redolent with the little details that seemed constantly to trigger little fantasies of Wyoming on his own turf. In the kitchen with a cup of tea , I imagined Turner, tall, with a lean swimmer's build, standing at the sink, Wyo coming up behind him and wrapping him in his big bear's arms. I imagined how it would feel to be Turner, sinking backward into that encompassing, manly softness. The mental movie led to Turner arching his neck to let Wyoming kiss it, and at the thought of how that beard must feel against the skin, I almost dropped my mug. Sitting in the living room one night, dawdling through a book, I just about passed out at the vision, sudden and unbidden, of Turner lying on top of his lover on the same couch I sat on. I could almost feel the heat of that huge, hairy body rising up into my own as I let the book slide to the floor, my hand slipping under my waistband and into my panties. Spreading my thighs and lying back against the leather, I sensed the room transformed in the soft yellow light, the couch an altar in a shrine to Eros, statues and feathered masks and ritual bells, naturally and inevitably surrounding it.

I imagined Turner and Wyo kissing, grunting as they stripped the clothes from one another's bodies, imagined watching Turner's hands, as worshipful as my own would be, caressing his lover's voluptuous bulk, fondling belly and thigh and hip as the two men's limbs tangled in passion. Eyes closed, I watched the scene unfold in my own mind as my fingers stroked my clit with short, sharp strokes: Turner on top, both of them writhing, hard cocks rubbing against each other as they kissed furiously, and then, as I geared up toward orgasm, the fleeting image of Wyoming turning the tables, using his weight to pin his slender lover to the leather cushions as he grabbed him by the hips and fucked him hard. The picture I conjured, Wyoming's huge hot ass clenching as he fucked his trembling lover, dwarfing him, covering him with his soft, strong, enormous body as he pounded into his ass, had me trembling too, writhing and biting my lip as I came and came again.

I was a little embarrassed about it, but I figured no one would ever know about it or the fantasies that filled my mind every time I went to the house. It got worse the longer I house-sat, the fantasies more vivid, the undertones of masculinity and sex that seemed to permeate the place harder to ignore. Partly it was simply the smell of Wyoming Smith himself, quite enough to make me feel faint. I had opened a closet door one evening while looking for an umbrella to get me home through a sudden rain, and the smell of that closet, when it hit me, was the closest thing I could imagine to what it would be like to actually be swept up in those massive arms: warm and musky, peat and cigar, hints of sweat and the dunglike smell of wet boots, mixed together with faint traces of spice and bits of bark. Standing in the doorway of a closet stuffed with field jackets and shirts, suitcoats and shoes, I flashed back to the first time Dr. Smith had leaned over me in seminar as I sat at the table with one of his hand-drawn maps of the Andes. He'd hovered over me, my petite frame insignificant next to the mountainous spread of his torso, and had felt my cunt clench involuntarily at the rich, dark smell of him, at the sheer presence of that much man.

So the smell was part of it. But only part—there was something about the house itself, particularly that living room, that seemed to put me instantly on the edge of an erotic daydream the second I sat on the couch or looked over the myriad objects on the tables and shelves. Perhaps they were partly to blame, too. No, scratch that. I *know* they were.

I knew, had known for some time through the campus grapevine, that one of Dr. Smith's hobbies was collecting arti-facts related to fertility cults and sex magic. Over the course of a week and a half, I'd managed to trace the origins and symbolism of many of the things I found scattered around the first floor— the terra-cotta *yoni* from God knows what crumbling tantric temple, an Etruscan satyr whose glazed clay hard-on had been pointing to the sky for centuries, humble clay Sheelagh-na-gigs spreading their cunts with both hands. There were any number of things either too humble or too esoteric for me to find documentation on, too, but it wasn't very hard to tell, what with the number of phallic symbols and stylized vaginas, what the idea behind the artifacts had been.

I was fascinated, professionally speaking. It was a crash course on something the university administration never would've let Wyoming teach, and I got to learn it very nearly at the master's hand. His hands! Oh, how I wished I could've learned at his big, strong hands, because the image of them haunted me. Every time I lifted one of the artifacts to look at it, I couldn't shake the notion of Wyoming's thick, sexy fingers having held and fondled it too.

That was precisely what I was thinking when I first spotted the goddess. It was the day before Wyoming was due home, and I was, frankly, indulging myself a little. It was private, it was warm, it was comfortable and well-furnished—everything my own ratty little room in the student ghetto across town was not. That it was Wyoming Smith's house only made it better. Having taken my hit of Wyo's downstairs closet, happily head-rushed on the concentrated smell of him, I sat there on that leather sofa, cradling a tiny, stone-studded clay doll in one palm, turning it over to find the disproportionately large cunt that had been poked into its fundament, and getting wet between the legs at the idea that Wyo's fingers had probed the very same hole that mine did.

The bulb in the lamp flickered and I looked up. It must have been a stroke of fate that made my gaze fall on her, tucked away on the bottom shelf, almost hidden behind an armchair, but once I'd seen her, I had to hold her. The little goddess was smooth and round, almost featureless except for slight creases of eyes and mouth and a tiny rise where her nose should have been, carved out of rippled tan agate, heavy and glassy in my hands. From the top of her head to the bottoms of her legs—she had no real feet—she was one long undulation. Her head a placid oval, her heavy breasts lay against a full belly, the subtle crease below it separating it from a mons that, even cut from stone, looked like a harem pillow.

I wondered what it would be like to look like that, rather than being short and having the kind of kid-like body—*elfin,* some people called it: no hips, tiny tits—that kept getting me carded despite the fact that I was twenty-nine. Her ass was luscious, her hips wide and round and full, and I wished her thick legs could open so that I could find out what kind of celestial cunt her sculptor would've given such a voluptuous creature. I held her in my hands, turned her and stroked her, marveling at how unutterably rich the little goddess was, about as tall as a Barbie doll but so much better, so much lusher, her curves so entrancing under my fingers.

She was turning me on.

She *was* turning me on, and it really was her, more even than the knowledge that she was Wyoming's, that was making me sigh and imagine what it'd be like to be with another woman as pillowy and unending and soft as the sleek, round goddess I held in my lap. My only experience with another woman had been with someone as skinny as me, and it had been a disappointment. She had even less of a butt than I did, and while her nipples were sensitive, there was precious little between them and the washboard of her rib cage. But it wouldn't be like that with someone like my goddess, I thought, my mind spinning out into visions of creampuff thighs and breasts bigger than my head, imaginary vistas of a belly soft and round enough to pillow me while I worked my hand inside her mythic wetness.

I leaned back, running the smooth, heavy statue across my belly, up over my breasts. Imaginary goddess-hands felt their way over my nipples, caressed the side of my neck, cool and heavy as they moved up and down my body, slowing as they seemed to concentrate on my thighs, coaxing my skirt up inch by inch as I moved the stone idol, letting my hands follow my fantasies.

A fleeting awareness of what I was doing flitted through my mind, then vanished amid mocha-tinted swells of flawless imaginary flesh. Lying on my professor's couch, running the smooth, hard head of what was probably a priceless artifact up and down over the damp crotch of my panties, I did honestly know what I was doing. I was quite aware that if anyone found out, they'd think I was crazy, or at least temporarily so. But no one needed to know, and I didn't care. My goddess felt so good, looked so good, her heaviness so perfect and her curves so lush, and I swear I could hear her in my mind, encouraging me with a low, ancient-sounding murmur of sheer pleasure.

She slid into me without hesitation as I moved my panties aside, her roundness seeming to know just how to slip between my drenched pussy lips, stretching and filling me with perfect hard weight. Eyes closed, I dreamt I felt her nipple beneath my lips, felt the sag of her breast as it flattened against my hip, the weight of her leaning against me as she fucked me thick and sweet. I stretched and shifted, pushing my hips up into my goddess's sweet long thrusts, a cascade of the goddess's hair falling across my face as I fucked up toward her. But her hair smelled of musk, somehow, and of beard and earth and cigars, and my breath quickened as she changed before me, metamorphosing against the backdrop of my closed eyelids, body changing shape, hands growing heavier, chest getting furry, arms beefier as they held my narrow shoulders down against the soft leather sofa. Pinned beneath the weight of him, I quivered breathless at the sensation of so much softness above me, around me, so much hardness inside me. I could smell his beard, smell the raw male-ness of him, furry tits dwarfing my own as he fucked me harder, deeper, meaty hips driving his cock into me again and again.

I clutched at him, clung to him, tried to bite his enormous arms, begged him to fill me, Wyoming above me on the expen-sive Italian couch, inside me to the hilt, blanketing me with his flesh, his mouth like sweet berries in a nest of ferns. Crazed with the weight, the thickness, the softness, the lust, I writhed beneath him, wrapped in the goddess's arms, feeling her smooth, fat form beneath me, her burgeoning breasts beneath my head, her sim-mering, voluptuous cunt bucking against my boyish little butt as Wyoming fucked me hot and tender, lush and true.

Alone again as my breath returned to normal, I pushed the Tibetan blanket that had fallen across my face back over the couch, blushing sheepishly at the mundane fact behind my poly-morphous fantasy. Sitting up, I held the agate goddess up to the lamplight. Glazed with my juices, bathed in my orgasms, she seemed almost to glow as I set her back on her shelf, lingeringly surveying her curves. I wondered, idly, where she'd come from, who had crafted her ageless, magical body, whether she was Etruscan or Minoan, Mayan or Indian. I wondered, *sotto voce,* whether in all the years she'd been around, she'd ever been used the way I'd just used her—then I laughed out loud.

Of course she had. Probably pretty recently, too. And I didn't have to be a Wyoming Smith to figure *that* out.

ALPHABET SOUP

Helen Bradley

A is for attraction, I felt it in the bar that night, your gaze swept the room, laser light flickering across your face. Your eyes traveled past mine, stopped, returned, met mine, up, down, up again. You smiled. Five years ago.

B is for bump. I still think it was deliberate, though you still say not. The bar, same night, I was angry then—for those few seconds before I realized it was you and that I could rearrange my face from "get away" into "oh, baby!" and shoot you a look that promised eternity if we could make it through the first date.

C is for cunt, your sweet cunt, moist with your come as I go down on you. Musky smell (I'll reuse that word again when I get to *M*), mmmm nice word, heady smell, my woman scent. Nah! I'm only teasing you, *C* is for coat, remember our first date? Remember how we courted each other, each unsure of the moves, sweetly romantic, so polite, hot and aching with desire underneath and covering it so well. *C* words: cunt, come, coat. Oh I forgot, it was cold as we returned to your car. You stopped, took off your coat, wrapped it around me and then wrapped yourself around it and kissed me, so gently, so softly under the street light. And stood back, your eyes dancing, a smile playing at the corners of your lips, deep breath and we continued on. Our first kiss.

D is for dyke. This one's a no-brainer, powerful word, reclaimed word, we call ourselves this in celebration of what we are. I watch as its edge catches people unaware and they hesitate, pause, did she say that? before they smile tolerantly (or not) and continue. Dyke, I want to yell, Dyke, Dyke, Dyke—it's what I am, for God's sake—I don't want pity, I don't want you to treat me as if it's a phase I'm going through. I just want to be me.

E. Eeek! I just realized that I messed up *B. B* is for butch. How can I have been so stupid? Wasted the letter *B* on the time you bumped me when it should have been butch. Strong big butch woman. Life partner, soulmate, lover, dyke. Shaven head, piercing, your smile, your stance, the way my heart leaps as you walk into the room. The way one look, one furtive sideways glance can register like a punch to my stomach and awaken deep inside me the urge to take your hand and lead you to bed. To have you pleasure my body, to press deep inside me, to fuck me until I scream for God. Why do we scream for God when we come? Even you, atheist that you are, you scream for him (or is it her?) as you come. Funny thing, I always think. You, butch lover, atheist, crying out for God. Always makes me smile, that does.

F. Well this one's a gimme, don't you think? Hey! I'm a dyke—I do it—I fuck. And I make love. There's a difference between them, don't you think? Two phrases, one raw and harsh, the other sappy and sweet. I want an "in between" word for what we do to each other. I ache for a word that has an edge that is powerful enough to explain what I feel when you strap on a harness and take me from behind, slamming into me until I scream. Oh, we covered the scream in *E,* didn't we? You know the words I cry out, I hear you say. Well, if you're so goddamn smart, then find me a word that puts the edge back on making love. I make love to you, you make love to me, we make love. From deep inside us springs love, celebrated every day we're together, every look, shared smile, every time your hand touches mine, when you wave me goodbye in the mornings, when you wink at me in the bathroom mirror as we brush teeth before bed and then achingly as your kisses trail down my belly and I open my legs for you.

G is for girth. Funny, old-fashioned word, but somewhere here in this alphabet soup of our lives I want to honor your size. Big, butch woman. I love your heavy hands, the thick fingers buried deep inside me. I love feeling your solid body fill my arms. I ache to have you on top of me, pressing your heavy weight into me. Imprinting my flesh as you have my mind and heart. And most of all? I like that you are proud of your body. When you came to me that first night, naked, seeking touch, desiring to pleasure me—I loved that you left the light on.

H. I'd say hair but there isn't much of it, is there? Perhaps head is better, and then I'll tell you how soft it feels to hold you near and run my cheek over the fine stubble that covers it as you tease my nipples.

I. This is a hard one. Can you help me here? No? OK, then perhaps I'll finish the rest and come back to *I* later.

J is for joker. The wild card in the pack. You're the joker in my life. You appeared that first night in my hand. I played you; I won the trick; I won the hand; I won my butch.

K. Kiss? *K* is definitely for kiss. Lots of different kisses. I love soft, gentle kisses on my lips, I love when you kiss my closed eyelids. I don't think nibbling my earlobe or pulling at my stud count as kissing, but in case I forget this by the time I get to *N* I'll put it in here. I love the hard, deep kisses you cover me with, in the heat of your passion, when you fuck my mouth with your tongue as you will so very soon fuck my body. Ohh...I love being kissed and I love kissing you at the point where your jaw meets your neck, and one nuzzling kiss is all it takes to force a ragged breath from you. The kisses I plant on you from behind as I wrap my arms around you as you prepare dinner, hoping that this will be one of the times you turn off the pot, put down the utensils, and give in to my desires and take me to bed. Mmm, I love kisses.

L. L would be for love if it weren't for life, but our love *is* for life. So *L* is for life and for the thanks I offer up to whatever greater being dumped us together in human form on this planet in the middle of some far-flung galaxy. Every day I live I give thanks for you in my life, for you *are* my life, my very being.

M is for musk. I remembered! See, you thought I'd get so carried away I'd forget my *M* word. But you forgot last night, you forgot that the taste of you is still on my tongue, you forgot that my face and hair were buried in your sex as I sucked you. You don't know that I haven't yet washed, and that if I stretch my tongue I can still find traces of you on my face to taste. If I move my head, the musky scent of you fills my nostrils yet again.

N. OK, OK...I remember this one too. Nuzzling, *N* is for nuzzling, or was it nibbling? Hey, what the heck—they both turn me on!

O. I hate to do this. I'm sorry, but I just had to. *O* is for Oh, those round-mouthed little cries you make just before you come that urge me on, telling me you're close. Then, when I take you that final step, you stop, silent, breath held, time suspended, until with a shudder you burst forth with a low groan as your body explodes in its release and I feel your contractions pulse through you.

P is for please. Not the "I please you and you please me" kind of please, but the urgent, begging please when I want you to take me when I can endure your teasing no longer and my body aches for your hand on my wetness. The urgent need I have for you that can only be satisfied by your hand or tongue, or, on those nights that you wear it, by your cock slamming into me.

Q is for quiet times. Those times we sit together in comfortable silence. When I curl up in the passenger seat as you drive, dreaming of new mountains to climb. When I sit back in your arms as we read our books nestled into each other. When I sit cross-legged for you to lie with your head on my legs half asleep, half awake, and I stroke your head: soothing, loving strokes. When we lie silently, each lost in our thoughts, replete from our lovemaking, together, always together, even in our separateness.

R is for roses. Anniversary roses for each year of our five years. Blood-red roses. Mine for you, yours for me. We merge the bunches, as we have merged our lives. One day each year we buy this visible symbol of the love we nurture on each of the other 364 days, until this day next year.

S is for skip. Cause I'm getting tired of this. Of watching you sitting opposite me, watching me. And me? Thinking all these things, when doing them is what I most want. So now I'm going to skip to the end of the alphabet really quick, and...

*T*ake you to bed and...

*U*ndress you...

*V*ery slowly, touching every inch of exposed flesh as I do, and...

*W*hen I have you undressed, butch woman—because this is what I most love to do—I will go down on you and fuck you with my tongue until you cry out for your release.

X marks the spot on your stomach where I start my trail of kisses toward your sex. If I start here, slowly, then by the time I reach my destination you will have pressed your legs apart, and the moisture of your arousal will glisten in the half light. Why does this always do it for you? I don't know, but I do remember I did it the first time you trusted me enough to let me go down on you, and how precious a gift I count it to be every time you allow me to repeat that journey.

Z. Zee end. Oh *puhleeze,* you say? No? OK, the *Z* is for the *zzz*'s and how I love watching you as you lie sated from our love-making, a small smile tickling your lips as you sleep...perchance to dream...of me.

DENIAL

Hanne Blank

Women. He wouldn't have been there at all if it hadn't been for women, Lou thought uncomfortably as he perched on the flimsy plastic seat of a folding chair. Above his head fluorescent bulbs complained nasally, just like Jessica used to every time Lou had so much as stirred a packet of sugar into his coffee.

"That's sixteen calories right there," Jessica would say, eyeing the empty sugar packet meaningfully. "Sixteen empty calories, Lou. I can't stand watching you eating yourself to death like this."

Mind you, Jessica hadn't always been like that. When Lou had first met her, she was a zaftig, juicy thing, all curves and jiggle, as creamy and luscious as a slice of freshly baked Boston Cream Pie. They were a matched set: two plump, dark Italians who both enjoyed baseball, science fiction, pizza, and, when Jessica was in the mood, some truly stellar sex. Lou still got a little dreamy remembering the way Jess's lush, compact body would writhe under him as she came, the shiver-inducing shimmy of her unthinkably soft, unthinkably generous breasts when he fucked her hard.

Then Jess got a promotion and a transfer, and started to worry about her corporate image. Lou didn't worry about corporate image. After all, he was a sysadmin—or, as Jess began to introduce him at her new departmental cocktail parties, "a senior-level Linux server guru"—and geeks at his level didn't need to have that front-office appearance. But Jess, who was gunning for another promotion, did. Or at least she thought she did. It all seemed innocent enough when she started going to the weekly Waist Whittlers® diet class that her company sponsored every Thursday after work.

Soon enough it was Mondays and Wednesdays and Thursdays, and sometimes a meeting on Sunday afternoons too. A couple of months, a $380 Waist Whittlers membership, and 32 pounds later (about $11.88 a pound, as Lou was fond of pointing out), Jessica was driving Lou crazy reciting the calorie count and fat grams of every single thing he put in his mouth. Existing on a handful of dog biscuit–sized vitamins and three miniscule vacuum-packed servings of Waist Whittlers Whittle Vittles™ each day, Jessica dwindled rapidly. Lou had been kind of relieved that the dieting made her less interested in sex, actually. As the lush curves he loved began to vanish, and considering the vicious mood swings she always went through when she dieted, he wasn't really all that interested himself.

Finally, Jessica dumped him. It wouldn't have been so bad, Lou thought, except that the next four women he'd hit on hadn't been interested in so much as grabbing a cup of coffee together, and the fifth, with whom he'd spent a few pleasant evenings, finally told him that she thought he was a great guy, but that physically, he just wasn't her type. Lou knew what that meant: Her type wasn't 341 pounds.

That was the measure of Lou's current adiposity, fresh from the official-looking, stainless-steel scale in the office where Lisa Reno, Waist Whittlers Certified Calorie Coach and Skokie Branch Manager, had slid the metal markers along the polished silver beams. Lou felt stupid and already chastened as he stood there in his stocking feet, but couldn't help but notice that Lisa Reno, in her bright yellow skirt and jacket, was really quite pretty, in a skinny sort of way. She also smelled good, clean and unperfumed, as she reached past his shoulder. Not that she'd be interested in the likes of him, Lou reminded himself. That was why he was in her office in the first place. As his hopelessly ecto-morphic coworker Matt had not-so-helpfully pointed out, girls seldom make passes at geeks with fat asses. That, Lou mused as he checked out the Calorie Coach's muscular legs, probably went double for girls who looked like they put in a fair bit of time on the stair machine and who worked in the fat farm trade.

Lou hadn't ever been exactly what he would've called thin, and he wasn't necessarily looking to get that way. His genetic background indicated stockiness, a broad chest, chunky thighs. But there was room for improvement, Lou told himself as he drove into the parking lot near the Waist Whittlers clinic, though he didn't have to go overboard like Jessica had. He used to get a lot of action back when he was about 250, 265. That was more what he was looking for.

And that, Lisa Reno assured him as she leaned across the corner of her desk and put her hand on his arm, was eminently possible—the Waist Whittlers way. "Lou, I'm so glad you came in to see me," she burbled brightly. "People like you who have a definite goal in mind are our biggest success stories here at Waist Whittlers. What I want to do as your Calorie Coach is to give you the support you need to take control of your life again, to be the man you want to be."

Lou thought Lisa Reno's hand had lingered on his arm maybe a fraction of an instant longer than really necessary, but then he was new to all this diet coach stuff. Waist Whittlers staff were supposed to be friendly and supportive, after all. It said so in the ads. Jessica had certainly found hers to be—she'd begun dating the guy who had been her Calorie Coach about thirty seconds after she'd given Lou the bum's rush. Lou rather suspected she'd been having Sven (of course he had to have some asshole name like "Sven," Lou thought) help her with some horizontal weight-loss techniques even before then.

From his vantage point in the middle of the back row of the Waist Whittlers conference room, Lou still thought it seemed as if Lisa Reno was paying him just a little more attention than entirely necessary. She was still businesslike and upbeat, and her attention was mostly on the brightly colored overheads she shone against the wall, but every once in a while she'd shoot Lou a short, enthusiastic little grin. It seemed a bit out of place, somehow, and Lou fidgeted, attempting gingerly to shift himself into a more comfortable position, cringing as the spindly metal-tubing legs of the folding chair wobbled beneath him. With great seriousness, he stared down at the photocopies he held, the same as the projections on the wall but in black-and-white, trying to conjure up some genuine enthusiasm for the charts of "free foods." The two plump mommy-types in the front row took notes in the margins of their handouts.

"With the green leafies, you can eat as much as you want, whenever you want, as long as you eat them plain. Those green leafy vegetables help keep you from feeling like you're denying yourself the chance to eat as much as you want any time you want," Lisa Reno explained, looking directly at Lou and smiling supportively. Was she trying to reassure him? Get a reaction out of him? Lou didn't know. The prospect of unlimited quantities of romaine lettuce wasn't exactly making him feel any better about this whole diet thing. Then Lisa Reno fumbled her transparencies, dropping one of them on the floor. Lou watched her pick it up, catching a glimpse down the front of her daisy-yellow jacket that made him wonder whether nipples were on the free foods list or not. You had to admit, Lou thought to himself, they'd beat the hell out of lettuce.

Discussion of free foods over, the neophyte dieters, overwhelmed with information and feeling more than slightly belittled in regard to the depth of their nutritional ignorance, took a break for cups of diluted tomato juice, some herbal tea, and their turn in the single seafoam-green bathroom. As Lou was about to leave the bathroom, he sized himself up in the full-length mirror on the back of the bathroom door. He'd been feeling pretty crappy since he walked into the place, but really he didn't look *that* bad. Maybe a little heavier than he'd like to be, he thought, but not bad. His dark hair was fairly recently cut, just long enough to let the wave show a bit, his eyes (his best feature, his first girlfriend had said) were big and dark and intelligent, his nose almost aristocratic, his moustache and goatee neatly trimmed. He squared his broad shoulders, and winked at himself as he retucked the front of his denim button-down, observing the little tuft of dark chest hair that showed just at the opening of the not-quite-buttoned-up shirt with an approving eye. Not bad. Looking his reflection up and down, he suddenly felt much better. He might be sitting in a Waist Whittlers meeting, he told himself firmly, but damned if he was going to let it make him feel as if he was just some stupid, lumpy schlub. He was fat, sure, but he had some pride.

Head held higher than it had been since he'd walked in, Lou returned to the conference room where Lisa Reno stood in her bright yellow suit, handing out cups of lukewarm

SuperHerbaTrim™ tea in little cups that bore the sprightly, athletic-looking Waist Whittlers logo. She smiled at Lou, a toothy, slightly goofy smile. What the hell, Lou thought to himself. If she wants to flirt, I'll flirt.

"I meant to tell you earlier," Lou said genially, accepting a barely warm cup from his brand new Calorie Coach, "how nice that suit looks on you. I was watching you during the lecture— you know, the free foods talk—and I just thought, well, you just looked very well put-together. Very sleek."

Lisa Reno blushed and beamed back at Lou, who was thanking his lucky stars he'd worked in his father's shoe store from the time he was thirteen until he graduated college to get the money to pay for his computer parts and software. The demands of schlepping loafers to middle-aged matrons had equipped him with social skills far beyond the ken of the average sysadmin, and flirting with their teenaged daughters while he fitted them in prom shoes had taught him the value of a compliment. Fat or not, he could still get 'em to blush and smile every time, and Lisa Reno was no exception.

The second half of the Waist Whittlers introductory meeting seemed to go by more quickly than the first half, a weird flutter of anticipation building in Lou's solar plexus as the hour passed. As Lisa Reno led the group through food-combining exercises and talked through the method of integrating Whittle Vittles™ meals into one's daily routine ("...simply replace one or two of the meals you would normally fix for yourself with these convenient, delicious meals and know that you are getting all the nutrition you need in a scientifically proportioned form that will help you lose weight even while you are eating," Lisa Reno recited, her voice hypnotizingly serene), she kept flashing glances at Lou, and on the occasions when he grinned back at her, he could've sworn she got a bit flustered.

By the end of the meeting, Lou was convinced she wasn't just being friendly. The smiles were too consistent, the glances too direct. She wasn't being professionally solicitous, either, he realized: He was the only one out of the eleven or so other Waist Whittlers newbies to whom she seemed to be paying much individual attention at all. It didn't really make sense, Lou thought, her being a diet instructor and him being a fat guy, but damned if it didn't actually seem as if she actually might be attracted to him, 341 pounds and all.

Like churchgoers paying their respects to the preacher, the dieters slowly filtered out to their cars, each of them stopping to say goodnight to Lisa Reno, who dispensed cheery smiles and encouraging words along with Belly Battler™ Beginner Boxes containing the first week's supply of Waist Whittlers Whittle Vittles. Duly armed against the demons of their appetites, the dieters meandered off into the cool Chicago night, leaving Lou and Lisa alone in the conference room. Lou hung back, pretending to examine some of the motivational magazines in the lucite wall rack. A few of the chubby chicks in the "before" pictures were pretty cute, he thought, flashing back for one wistful moment to the yielding satin of Jessica's former hips. Out of the corner of his eye, he eyed Lisa Reno's flat-tummied, gym-toned frame, and imagined how her slight, adamantly firm hips might feel by comparison. He hadn't ever really gone for Lisa's physical type. Gym babes just seemed kind of…well…vapid, most of the time, and not nearly as sexy as round girls. But, Lou rationalized, if he was going to lose weight, he guessed it wouldn't be a bad thing to date a skinny woman for a while. It'd be good reinforcement. And besides, Lisa Reno had been making eyes at him for an hour and a half, and who was he, 341-pound Lou Giantonio who hadn't been able to get his fat self laid in six months, to look a gift horse in the mouth? Maybe if he made progress between now and next week he'd ask her out.

"So, anyway," Lou said, walking slowly up to the table where the last remaining Belly Battler Box sat waiting for him, "I just thought I'd say thanks for the encouragement, and I guess I'll see you in a week, Miss Reno."

"Oh, please, call me Lisa," she replied, her hands nervously fondling the corners of the box that lay on the table between them. "I hate being called Miss Reno, it seems so formal. Besides, as your Calorie Coach, I really am more of a friend, you know. A confidante. I'm here to help."

"Well, thanks, then, Lisa," Lou said, grinning. "So, anyway, I guess this box here is all I need, right?"

"Yep, that's your first week, right there, the good old Belly Battler." She patted the box as if it were a favorite old dog. "Starting tomorrow morning, all you have to do is work the Plan. And don't forget those free foods. They can really help, if you start to feel deprived."

"Yeah, I bet." Lou had never really liked lettuce all that much.

"Deprivation's no fun. That's why I think this system is so good, you know? You'll be amazed—you really won't feel like you have to live in a constant state of self-denial, not at all. All you have to do is follow the Plan." Lisa looked deep into Lou's eyes as she said this, her mouth on autopilot, her gaze absolutely rapt.

Damn, Lou thought. She really *was* interested. "So what does the Plan say you should do on the night before you start?"

Slightly surprised, Lisa admitted that there wasn't really a standard thing dieters were supposed to do the night before they started their Waist Whittlers program. Then she paused and looked down at her hands, examining the neatly filed tips of her nails for a moment. Then she looked up, her voice a bit gentler, more genuine, than it had been before. "Well, I haven't had dinner yet. Care to join me, since you're not on the Plan yet? It can be tough going out, once you're on the Plan, but hey, you're not there yet, right?"

Lou chuckled, then nodded. "Like the Romans used to say, 'Eat, drink, and be merry, for tomorrow you shall diet?' Sure, I'm game. I actually haven't had dinner yet either. My car's here, though. How 'bout we meet up at Lou Malnati's?"

Their destination set, Lou grabbed his Belly Battler Beginner Box and Lisa Reno turned out the lights and locked the doors. Tossing his box of diet food and pamphlets into the passenger seat, Lou slid behind the wheel of his Volkswagen and cranked up the CD player as he started the engine. With Zappa's *Yellow Shark* blaring from the speakers, Lou drove toward the restaurant, thumping his plump fingers on top of the Belly Battler box in time with the music and thinking how ironic it was that he seemed to be in the process of pulling a Jessica—his first day in Waist Whittlers, and his Calorie Coach had already asked him out to dinner. Now that, Lou thought with a chuckle, was what you called comprehensive customer service.

In the restaurant, Lou and Lisa chatted amicably, making small talk and sipping glasses of red wine while they waited for their food to arrive. She'd encouraged Lou to order whatever he wanted, her encouragement so enthusiastic that he'd raised an eyebrow at her.

"Odd to have my Calorie Coach encouraging me to eat like this," he remarked. "My ex-girlfriend—I mentioned her to you, she dropped a ton of weight on Waist Whittlers—was always after me about what I ate. Forgive me if I'm a little surprised."

"Sounds like your ex-girlfriend went a little off the deep end," Lisa replied with a knowing smile. "I see that happen a lot. No, I'm not about starving yourself or depriving yourself. See, the way I see it, denying yourself is the worst thing you can do when you're talking about a lifestyle change program like Waist Whittlers. It makes you feel like a bad person, like you don't deserve good things. And, you know, that just sabotages you, because losing weight and getting healthy are good things, right?"

Lou nodded cautiously. Something about Lisa Reno wasn't feeling kosher to him, but he couldn't quite put his finger on it yet.

"So I think it's actually really good for you to eat whatever you want—no matter what it is—before you start the Plan tomorrow. That way, you won't go into it feeling like denial is going to be part of the whole experience. I mean, I'm going to have a salad. They have great salads here, and I love salad. Eat it all the time. And if you're really in the mood for a salad, I'm not about to stop you. But honestly, order whatever you want."

In the end, Lou had shrugged and taken her at her word. Having missed lunch because some idiot in a branch office had hosed the password file on one of the machines he administered, he was pretty starved. Maybe a good dinner really would help him feel better about starting his diet in the morning.

Lisa seemed like a fairly OK sort, Lou thought as the waiter set his plate of mostaccioli in cream sauce down in front of him. They'd chatted about their jobs, about Chicago and commuter traffic, and then she'd mentioned how nice it was that her VCR was set to tape *Ally McBeal* so that she wouldn't have to miss it, because she certainly was enjoying getting to know Lou a bit better. It made Lou smile and blush a bit, for while Lisa Reno didn't necessarily seem like the kind of woman he'd ever want to settle down with, she certainly seemed genuinely interested, which was more than had happened with anyone else since Jessica had taken off for leaner pastures.

At the same time, there was something just a little odd about Lisa, and Lou still couldn't quite figure out what. She seemed warm and friendly, and she did seem both honestly attracted to him as well as genuinely interested in what he had to say. She was pretty, too, in a sort of cookie-cutterish way. But something bothered him.

After half a plate of pasta, it dawned on him. Lisa was watching every mouthful he ate. Not like Jessica had, though. That was the weird thing. Lisa's eyes lit up every time Lou lifted a forkful to his lips, and even though she barely did more than pick at her salad, she licked her own lips with unconscious satisfaction every time he chewed and swallowed. A bit confused, Lou watched her watching him, her voyeuristic enjoyment becoming more and more obvious with every bite he took.

He had to ask. But it wasn't as if he could just come out and say it. That would be rude, and besides, it was a little weird. She might get embarrassed, or offended. Maybe she was just staring at him in general, and she simply didn't know how to break the ice, and it only seemed like she was watching him eat. Lou didn't want to presume too much. And he certainly didn't want to ruin his chances with her. She might be a little unusual, but after all, she *was* interested.

"So, ah, Lisa…" he began, setting down his water glass, "pardon me if I'm being too nosy or anything, but, er…well, I'm just curious: What makes a slim, attractive, health-conscious lady like yourself interested in a guy like me, anyway?"

Lisa blushed becomingly, giggling nervously into her wineglass as she drained it. "Oh, hell, Lou, you seemed like an interesting guy, I guess. I don't meet a whole lot of men in my line of work, you know? Mostly it's women who come into Waist Whittlers. And you're so smart, and, well, I don't know. Is it OK if I just think you're interesting?"

"I suppose," Lou said, with an affable, sheepish smile. He felt embarrassed. Why should there have been anything more to it than that? Now he'd probably offended her, made her feel as if he didn't trust her or something. He tried to make up for it, cracking a few jokes as he ate a bit more of his dinner, but he still felt kind of lame. Fortunately Lisa was adept at carrying a conversation more or less single-handedly, which she did without skipping a beat. She still stared at him while he ate, but Lou tried to just let it be, tried to accept that it was just that she thought he was attractive, even if it didn't quite feel as if that was all there was to it.

Out in the parking lot after dinner, Lou walked Lisa to her car, a green Lexus with a "Waist Whittlers® WORKS" bumper sticker. It was a company car, she explained proudly, and she'd earned it by being one of the top ten sellers in the Chicagoland area two years in a row. Then her voice dropped, and she moved a little closer to Lou, who stood with his hands in his pockets in the slightly chilly night air.

"Well, thanks, Lou," she smiled softly, looking up slightly to gaze directly into his eyes, "I've had a lovely time hanging out with you tonight. Look, I hope I'm not being too forward or anything...."

"No, not at all, Lisa," Lou hastened, reflexively reassuring. Her gaze felt hungry (and probably was, Lou figured, since she hadn't seemed to eat much) as it met his. The force of the desire in her expression, her lips slightly parted and her eyes so intently focused, left Lou momentarily speechless, not knowing how he could possibly respond. When she leaned in a bit further, he blinked once or twice and then suddenly realized that Lisa Reno, Waist Whittlers Certified Calorie Coach and Skokie Branch Manager, was kissing him full on the lips.

She was kissing him quite passionately, in fact, and almost in spite of himself he was kissing her back, the sudden sweet softness of her lips against his making his skin prickle with the pleasure of brand-new desire. She snuggled up against him, her hands lightly moving to his shoulders, and Lou sighed a reflexive sigh of sheer sensual relief. It felt so good to be touched, to be wanted, and when one of Lisa's hands slipped off his shoulder and down his back, he reached for her and pulled her to him hard, pressing her and her yellow suit against the ample curve of his belly.

Lisa gasped into his mouth, their tongues twisting and exploring, Lou relishing the thought that she could be so into him, hardly daring to believe it was so. He ran his fingers through her short bob, letting her nuzzle his neck, grinning as she nibbled his goatee and he glided his hand over her hip. It wasn't so bad, he thought. She felt different, sure, maybe not as soft as he'd ideally like, but who was he to complain when she was so damned eager? Tugging her hip toward his own, Lou grinned inwardly at her enthusiasm. His cock was swelling in his boxers, and his heart was beating a little faster than he might've wanted to admit. Jessica hadn't been like this with him since before she'd gotten her promotion. It felt damned good. It had been too long since he'd felt as if anyone cared...that anyone wanted him, that way.

Suddenly they broke apart, aware that they were standing in a public place. Still wrapped in one another's arms, they blushed and laughed and looked around themselves, afraid they'd made a scene. It was late, though, and the parking lot was mostly empty, so with a wry little shrug, Lou leaned forward and kissed Lisa on the forehead.

"Wow," he breathed, looking at her incredulously.

"Yeah, definitely wow," she agreed, leaning her head on his shoulder and nuzzling his neck. "I'm glad...I mean...I'm glad you don't think I was being too pushy or anything."

"Not at all. It's kind of nice, really. It's been a while."

"Really? I wouldn't have expected that," Lisa murmured as she let her lips graze the corner of Lou's jaw.

"No, really. I mean, it's not like I have women chasing me down the street. Most women don't really…well, you know…go for guys who are…"

"Handsome? smart? funny?" Lisa teased, interrupting him.

"No, but thanks for the compliment. I meant that most women don't really go for guys who are fat." Stating it that baldly felt a little strange, but it also somehow felt necessary, something that needed to be said. Lou felt himself blush slightly, his cheeks flushing with a warmth that had nothing to do with Lisa's lips.

"Their loss, I'd say," Lisa said softly as she straightened up. Looking slightly worried, she pushed her hair back behind her ear and watched Lou's expression for a moment. "I mean…well, it's kind of complicated."

"What is?"

"I dunno. I mean, I like big guys. Guys who are built like you. Fat guys, I guess. I always have. I think you're amazingly sexy, honestly. I should've been more honest with you when you asked me earlier, I guess." Lisa looked slightly scared as she spoke, biting her lip for an instant before she continued. "You just turn me on. A lot. And like I said, in my job I don't actually get to meet all that many men…."

"Hey, at least in your job, the ones you meet are more likely to be ones you actually think are hot," Lou joked, feeling a little weird. Humor seemed to be the only way to respond, but it didn't really feel very funny.

Lisa smiled a relieved smile. "Yeah. My dirty little secret. It's the best perk of the job." She patted the side of her car affectionately. "Well, aside from the Lexus."

Lou stepped back and leaned against the side of the car, not really responding much when Lisa sidled up alongside him, pressing lightly against his firm, fleshy side. "So, uh, you're a Calorie Coach with a thing for fat guys. Huh. Who would'a thunk it?"

Lisa blushed. "Yeah, I know. But I *like* what I do. I think it's important. I mean, it feels kind of weird sometimes, but you know, it really is better being thinner. I used to be thirty pounds heavier, and trust me, you're just a lot healthier when you're thin. So I mean, really, I'm providing a public service. Just because I think it's sexy doesn't mean it won't still kill you, you know? And some guys are still really sexy when they're thinner. Not *as*, but, you know, you make sacrifices. Life's so much easier for people when they get on the Plan and lose the weight. You'll see."

Something was churning inside Lou, and only part of it was the pasta and breadsticks he'd eaten, which had begun to act like they'd just had a quick samba lesson from the dance studio on the far side of the parking lot. Lou felt…he wasn't quite sure what he felt. Lisa's lust seemed so sweet, but her rationalizations just sounded weird. He didn't get it. Not knowing what else to do, he nodded. After a moment, he spoke. "So what is it that you *like* about fat guys?"

Lisa got a curious little-girlish expression on her face for a moment as she reached out, gingerly putting her hand on the top-most curve of Lou's full, heavy belly. Her palm and fingers felt warm, almost hot through the cotton of his shirt, and Lou felt his cock stirring involuntarily. "Softness, I guess, for one thing. But at the same time, the size is so sexy, so…weighty. Significant. Some big guys seem just so much more masculine than thin guys. You're like that. Something about the way it makes you walk. You take up space. It's imposing. Powerful. I love that. I love looking at a big guy who's built like you and…well…imagining what it might feel like to be underneath him…pinned down under him."

Anger battled with arousal as Lou listened to Lisa talk, as he watched her dreamy expressions and felt her hands on his body. Part of him was raging, a strange and primal sense of betrayal electrifying his thoughts. How dare she? How fucking well dare she talk like that, be so bald-faced as to tell him he was good enough for her libido but too fat for her world? Yeah sure, his belly was good enough for her to drool over in a parking lot, but she'd still sell him a fucking truckload of those goddamned Belly Battlers if it'd get her another Lexus. She'd probably rather eat a pound of rock salt than swallow an extra fat gram, but she'd ask him out to dinner and get wet watching him eat pasta with cream sauce. And she wanted him. She was stroking his belly. Her fingers were trailing the top of his waistband, dipping below his belly and stroking so close to his pubic hair line that it made him gasp out loud in spite of himself.

Then, suddenly, Lou thought how weird it must be to be her, to lust after fat men so much that just watching him eat made her breathless, meanwhile dedicating her life to making people thinner, earning a living by making the thing she found hotter than anything else in the world literally vanish. How awful, he thought, letting himself get lost for a moment in the sensation of her hands caressing his sides. How awful for her.

Then she squeezed him, holding double handfuls of his flesh in her strong fingers, grabbing his fat hard enough that it hurt a bit. "Gonna be kind of sad to watch this sexy stuff go," she murmured against his chest, jostling the handfuls of flesh she held. "But it's for your own good. You'll still be cute, you know. You really do have *such* a pretty face." The anger flashed back instantly, scathing torrents of outrage seeming to flow from the spots on his sides where her hands grasped his flesh. Lou took a deep breath. Fucking hypocrite bitch.

Lou put his hands on Lisa's arms, his warm, firm fingers sliding down her forearms to her wrists. Holding them loosely, he took them away from his belly, backing her up against the side of her Lexus. She looked up at him demurely, passively, eyes glittering with excitement, her mouth opening in a soft *O* of arousal.

Lisa's lips were puffy and dark as Lou held her against the car, leaning over her, his big heavy belly pressing her against the cold glass and metal.

"So this is what you like about fat guys, huh, Lisa?" Lou's voice was low, and it rumbled in his chest in a way that sent vibrations all the way up—and down—Lisa's arched-back spine. "You like the idea of this big, fat, solid belly pressing you down, not letting you move until I'm done with you, don't you?"

Lisa gasped, speechless, nodding. In the dim parking lot, it looked almost as if her eyes were watering with need. Lou wedged her thighs open as far as her tight knee-length skirt would allow, pressing his own wide leg between them. It was all completely clear to him, the anger and betrayal he felt seeming to crystallize into a single, white-hot kernel in his solar plexus.

"You like it when all this soft, powerful, masculine flesh just drapes all over you, don't you? Yeah, that's what you like. Someone this much bigger than you, this much heavier than you, to just hold you down and give it to you. I bet you want to have your hands all over me right now, don't you, Lisa? I bet you want to pull me on top of you, knead all this softness, feel it, grab it, have it all for yourself. Don't you?"

A soft, vaporous *ohyesplease"* floated from Lisa's lips, her knees buckling slightly as Lou leaned into her, grinding his thick thigh against her crotch.

"Don't think I can't smell how wet you are, Lisa."

She turned crimson, blushing so hard that it was obvious even in the half-dark. She tried feebly to close her legs, but Lou's meaty thigh held them apart.

"No, you don't," he chastised, flashing her a glittering, indulgent smile. "Not until you tell me how much you want it. You do want it, don't you, Lisa? You want this hot, fat body on top of you. You want to feel three hundred and forty-one pounds of sheer man pounding into you while you grab big handfuls of me and feel how soft I am in your hands. You can't hide from me, Lisa. I know you want it."

Lisa was nodding nonstop, murmuring *yes* again and again, her hips grinding in slow arcs against Lou's solid, implacable thigh. "Please, Lou," she whimpered as he readjusted his grip on her wrists, the gesture reminding her that he had her pinned, just the way she wanted it. "Please. Let's go to my place, OK? God, you're so fucking hot. I want it. Just exactly like that. I want it so fucking much."

Somewhere in Lou's belly the kernel of anger burst, a white explosion so strong that he closed his eyes for a second. Opening them again, he leaned in to Lisa's face, stopping when his lips were a mere fraction of an inch above hers as she panted hoarsely underneath him.

"Yeah, Lisa. That's right, you want it," he growled in a hoarse bass voice. "You want this big fat man to fuck you blind, don't you?"

Lisa just groaned, her eyes pleading.

"Say it, Lisa. Tell me you want this big fat body. Tell me how much you want it."

Lou's blood flashed in his veins, adrenaline and anger, arousal and amazement at his own voluptuous cruelty making every nerve in his body sing. It was an effort for her to say it, but she did, her voice cracking with lust. "I...I want your fat fucking body, Lou. I want you to fuck me so bad. I want it."

Pressing into her hard, almost crushing her between his body and the side of her car, Lou regarded her for an instant, then shook his head. With infinite slowness, he finally spoke.

"You can't have it."

Dropping her arms abruptly, Lou stepped away from the trembling yellow-suited Calorie Coach as she clutched at the side of her shiny Lexus to keep from slumping to the ground. Her face was thunderstruck, petrified with incomprehension.

"You're a hypocrite, Lisa Reno," Lou said calmly as he walked away. "And you can't have it."

Back in his car, Lou turned the CD player on as he rolled down the windows and started the engine. He felt clean somehow, refreshed, the spot inside him where the rage had been as serene and pure as a goddamned afternoon in the country. Lou didn't bother to look back as he peeled out of the parking lot. He just reached for the box on the passenger seat, grabbed it by its convenient carrying handle, and pitched it out the open window, the angular rhythms of Zappa's "G-Spot Tornado" ensuring that he would never know the sound a Belly Battler Beginner Box made as it smashed to pieces on the pavement.

FLESH LOVE

Debra Hyde

Her thighs are lush and large, and between them lie mysteries as dark and wet as the depths of an African jungle. I survey every inch of her as if it were an acre of dense foliage, and, like an explorer who has come to be awed and not to conquer, I wish I could lose myself completely in this land, never to return to civilization. This land of hers, this hot skin that quakes at my every touch, that responds to my fingertips, that comes alive at the tip of my tongue, beckons me upward and inward.

I kiss every dimple I meet as I travel north from her knees. I knead her flesh, hoping to memorize the beauty of the path I'm traveling, hoping never to forget the journey once the journey's done.

I nibble at her, tasting the succulence of her skin, marveling at the fullness of her body.

I worship her.

She moans now, aroused. Wild marvels call to me.

Did unnamed creatures beckon to explorers from within the dark jungles of old Africa the way the sirens called to Ulysses' men? Who knows, but they call to me in her moans, these sounds that rumble from the depths of her and tell me to come to her, to part her ways with my tongue, to find the rich rewards. They tell me to plunder her rich bounty, to find that exquisite nugget, to claim it.

But I know I never really claim anything. I know that, as I work my way to her moist, musty interior, I come out of awe, in reverence for her wild beauty.

I come to worship.

And when I snake my way between her thighs, when my tongue finds her sweet slit, I lose myself in the smell and taste of her beauty, a beauty that's wet with lust, a beauty that grinds into my face, a beauty that, when it peaks, fiercely crushes me between her thighs. Blood rushes in my head, I gasp for air, and all I know in that moment is her scent, her pulse, her power.

I wish she'd never let go of me.

• • •

How did I meet Jack? Blind date. No, no fooling, and when I first saw him, I thought, "Oh no! No, no, no, no, no!" I mean, he looked like a 99-pound weakling—you know, like the guy in those old Charles Atlas ads who got the sand kicked in his face?—and I couldn't have that. I mean, really, with my plumpness? What would I tell friends? "Hi, this is my boyfriend, Jack Sprat. You know, as in 'eat no fat'?"

Except the first time he ate my fat, I died and went to heaven. Yeah, I know—why sleep with the guy if I thought he was such a dork? What can I say? He looked helpless, and I pitied him. At least I waited until the third date.

Only I found he wasn't helpless after all, just afraid he'd never be able to help himself to me. Imagine my surprise when the dork turned out to be a genius in bed.

I learn something new every day.

So now I don't care if we're Jack Sprat who could eat no fat, and his wife could eat no lean. Besides, it's not true—he eats fat just fine, and I love the lean cuisine that's between his legs.

• • •

Some people use the word *Rubenesque* to be kind. At one time, I used it reverently, like an acolyte divining the great mysteries of his religion. But with her, Rubenesque has no meaning. She is beyond that, greater than that. Larger than that. She is huge, ripe, full of life and fertility. She is like an Olmec earth mother, all flesh and fat, breasts ready to feed the world, loins capable of birthing humankind.

And it is the Olmec lover whom I worship.

I worship her when she beckons me to her backside, flashing a slit of pink before closely her legs tightly and telling me to "Try and find it." I come to her, my pants at my ankles, my shirt-tails hanging—crude, I know—and let my cock fish its way into her. Often, she coos. Always, she's wet and ready.

Her backside hides her wilderness from me. I ache because I can't see it, even though it teases me—wafting its rich aroma up to me, enveloping me in its slick, wet depth. That wilderness drives me wild, makes me primitive.

When I look down and see my cock go at her, I watch it disappear into her, fully, completely, and I realize I'm such a little thing compared to her vastness. I start thinking all sort of Freudian thoughts, thoughts of her cunt suddenly snapping shut and biting off my penis and claiming it for its own.

I imagine her cunt chewing it up, swallowing it, and never giving it back. Or worse—spitting out the pieces just to prove it can.

Sometimes I feel like a Lilliputian to her Gulliver, just waiting for her to rise up from bondage and squash me, but even when she's on all fours, my Olmec lover towers over me.

• • •

Oh, God, you should see the ways I make Jack come. I'm not kidding the man is such a little perv. Hey, you remember Kevin, that kid who always stared at my chest in high school? Remember that time I caught him ogling and I pushed my tits together and yelled, "Hey Kevin, is the view better this way?" Remember how he turned beet-red and then went pale? You know, I bet he creamed in his pants. Anyway, Jack can be like that.

I used to think stuff like that was sick, but the first time I showed Jack my breasts, he looked just like that kid Kevin, all embarrassed and in agony. Plus, his cock went instantly hard and all oozy. I discovered I really like making him feel that way. I enjoy having that kind of power over him.

Sometimes when we're naked, I gather my breasts up in my hands and push them together, then have him stick his dick in between them. You know, he can fuck pussy all day long without coming, but you give him tits to fuck and he shoots in thirty seconds flat.

Want to know how I learned about his big-breast fetish? Yeah? Well, once when I was on top—and this was after fucking for God knows how long and I came for, like, the fifth time—I couldn't take it anymore and I collapsed onto him. My tits landed square on his face and I heard this muffled gasp underneath me. I figured I should get up, but he pulls me closer and holds me there. So I push my weight down on him and the next thing I know, he's coming and screaming into my breasts. God, it was so hot.

I guess that makes me a pervert, too.

• • •

Her breasts give life, and her breasts can take it away. She can offer them to me, nudging me to latch onto her wide, inviting nipple, allowing me to suckle as if my life depended on it. Or she can squash me beneath them, robbing me of breath while giving me the ecstasy of oblivion.

I don't know which of the two I like better.

When I come to her breast, like Romulus or Remus to the she-wolf, I feel nurtured, guarded, protected. I am a lover child, in awe of mother's raw womanhood. I am the beneficiary of breasts that could cradle the world in their cleavage. When her nipple grows hard in my mouth, when I reach to her and touch her breasts, I feel as if I'm touching the fount of mankind. I feel blessed.

Yet when her breasts crush me, I'm rendered delirious, abjectly so. Her breasts are heavy weights, globes that make me quiver and place me at her mercy. They suck the breath from me as the scent of her body overwhelms my senses. When I'm under their power, I know only her existence—her crushing, over-whelming existence.

And just when I begin gasping, that's when it happens—that's when her very essence sucks my masculinity from me. My cock loses all composure and comes. Her breasts force the life from my cock; her breasts make it gasp its last, regardless of where it is and what it's doing.

When she hears me come, she rises from me, leaving me humbled and gasping for air. Then I am at my most vulnerable and weak. I am incapable of anything. That is when the Olmec earth mother redeems me. She brings her teat of sustenance and renewal to me. Then, I close my eyes, latch on, and find comfort.

Earth's bounty, given to me.

• • •

You know what really takes my breath away? The way Jack worships me. I mean, I bet he'd literally kiss the ground I walk on if I told him to. At first, I found it a little embarrassing, but as I got to know him, I really grew to love it. He makes me feel like a goddess.

And talk about *changing* me! Well, I mean he hasn't *changed* changed me, but he *has* introduced me to all sorts of hot sex stuff and—jeez Louise, if I'm not getting wet panties every time I think about getting naked with that man.

You know what? After we're done with lunch here? I'm going to meet him at his office. I'm going to go shut the door to his office, unbutton my blouse as I go right up to him, and press my tits into his face. No friendly kisses, no casual chat, just my tits in his face.

And I'm going to keep them there until he's gasping for air. I'm going to talk dirty to him. I'm going to tell him how wet I get while I'm crushing my breasts into him and how unfair it is that I'm the only one who's wet. I'm going to tell him that I won't lift my breasts from his face until he has a wet spot on his pants to match the one between my legs.

I wonder if he'll come. I wonder if *I* will.

When we're done, I'll stand up and button my blouse and look for that wet spot on his pants. And then, when I look into his face, I know I'll see that look there, the one that shows he's the luckiest man on earth, as if he can't believe his good fortune and he's so damn thankful for it.

When I see that look, I melt. I bet I respond with a certain look of my own. I bet it says, "Works both ways, Buster."

IN SEASON

Corbie Petulengro

Kitty came to Rein's farm at the bottom of a long, slow fall off a cliff. Actually, "washed up at Rein's farm" was more like it. Dropped off in the driveway by a friend who sped back to the city in a cloud of dust, she stood like a waif on Rein's doorstep, among the tinkling sun-and-star wind chimes, and begged for sanctuary. Rein just stood there and looked at her for a moment, said, "Wait here," and walked off into the house.

Kitty looked helplessly at Gabriel, Rein's sometime lover, a delicate, lean, long-haired slip of a man barely taller than Kitty herself. He leaned against the door lintel, clad in cutoffs and a frilly lavender blouse—Gabriel cross-dressed a lot at home—and grunted laconically to her around the joint clenched in his teeth. "She's gone to check the cards."

"What?" Kitty tried to look charmingly bewildered, instead of stupidly so. It wasn't easy, as frazzled as she felt.

"The tarot. She'll do a reading and decide whether or not you can stay beyond the three-day guest-right. We never deny that to anyone." He took the joint out of his mouth and held it out to her; she shook her head, unsure whether she should be pissed off. Her fate rested on some tarot reading being performed somewhere else in the house. The thought was not comforting.

Then suddenly Rein appeared again, jerking her head toward the inside of the house. "You can stay."

Kitty never did find out what the cards had said, but very soon it didn't matter, because she was in Rein's warm kitchen with dinner smells emanating from the antique woodstove, copper kettle whistling with tea. It was like having stepped back in time; being at Rein's always was, a very different world than that of Kitty the urban club-hopper. She felt the odd sensation of having landed with a thud, an almost audible sound, the impact at the bottom of the cliff. Even if she wasn't exactly on her feet, she was at least safe. Temporarily.

Lots of other people lived on Rein's farm, most of them wandering or disaffected queers who had washed up on its green rural shore, tucked away in the shadow of Mount Wachusett. Gabriel was one, and there were others, although not too many this time, which was why Kitty managed to get a real room instead of merely a fold-out couch. She would remember the others later as vague presences who might be interesting to talk to over the morning coffee, but who always seemed to vanish when Rein entered the room. No matter who else lived there, no one ever called it anything but Rein's Farm.

Rein, pronounced *Rine,* was short for Reinhold, which was short for C. Reinhold Gunnarsen. Kitty never did find out what the C was short for, but it was probably something far too feminine. Rein was a butch, but she was absolutely nothing like any of the butches who James Dean'd around the bars, offering to light Kitty's cigarettes or buy her drinks or fistfuck her. She knew how to handle them, how to flirt and toss her hair and make them blush or pant or temporarily lose motor control. They were easy, so desperate for a femme to help them prove their butchness, to feel their muscles and watch them pump iron, to nestle behind them on their motorcycles and ruffle their crew cuts. Easy.

Too easy. Too easy to forget that someone full of insecurity could sometimes explode, could sometimes sense manipulation like an animal smells the butcher's knife behind the food bowl, and lash out. That was why Kitty was hiding, three hundred miles from home, with a matching set of black eyes.

Rein was a whole different kind of ball game. She was butch without even trying. Maybe it was because she worked a butcher job than all the city girls and simply didn't need to prove anything. She didn't swagger, she was simply competent. When something needed fixing, she did it, whether it was pancakes or a tractor engine. She was 250 pounds of flesh in a flannel shirt and a sheepskin vest, and you couldn't tell how much of that was muscle and how much was fat. All you knew was that her muscles came from heaving bales of hay, not from a Bow-Flex. She wore boots almost all the time, but they were manure-caked, not shiny from someone's loving care, and instead of a crew cut she wore her waist-length flaxen hair in two braids. On anyone else it would've looked ridiculous, while on Rein the effect was like that of a warrior queen from some Viking saga.

Nothing Kitty did had ever worked on Rein. The woman was completely unmoved by flirtations and ploys. The few times Kitty'd met Rein at parties given by mutual friends, Kitty had been first annoyed by that, and then somehow strangely tremulous. The truth was that Rein scared her. So, of course, when Kay had turned violent, Kitty had instinctively fled to her doorstep. If she frightens me, her unconscious seemed to argue, then she's certainly tough enough to handle Kay.

And it wasn't as if she really wanted Rein, anyway, not that way. The woman was....well, *wide.* Kitty had never touched anyone whose belly burgeoned over their belt in that way. Or whose thighs were the size of Kitty's waist. Or, certainly, any butch whose breasts were bigger than hers. No, she just wanted to hide in the protection of Rein's massive shadow until the danger was over. A tree, Kitty thought—I'll just think of her as a big gnarled oak tree in whose green branches I can be safe. Not as a breathing, fleshy human being, just a tree.

After all, she wasn't Rein's type any more than Rein was hers. She knew because Rein had told her so at one of those parties, when Kitty had been almost reflexively flirting with everyone there. "You aren't my type," Rein had said, offhandedly. As if that was why she'd been doing it, as if she had actually been interested in the big woman.

"So what *is* your type?" Kitty asked, feeling nettled. She already knew that Rein was bisexual.

The Viking warrior frowned and bit the end of the pencil she'd been messing with. "Tougher," she said finally. "Less fragile." Then she added, as a parting shot, "More competent. Good for something."

A thousand retorts had died unsaid in Kitty's mouth as she realized that to defend herself might be to imply an interest in Rein. In the end, the fact that she'd kept her mouth shut had been the proof of how much the woman intimidated her. That, and she had to admit she wasn't sure what she'd have said to prove that she was actually good for something. It was a long time before she admitted to herself how deep that barb had penetrated.

• • •

It must have been that urge to be protected that had her trailing
Rein around from barn to woodshed to workshop over the next
several days, trying to engage her in conversation. It wasn't that
Rein wouldn't talk. She was quite articulate and self-educated,
and willing to hold forth on a number of subjects. It was just that
she expected Kitty to talk and work at the same time. "Hold this,"
she'd say, or "Put that up there for me," and suchlike. Or, on one
occasion, "Go into the stall and hand me the sheep water bucket."

"But there's two inches of manure in there," Kitty objected.

"So?" Rein's voice came from inside the goats' stall. "You
can clean your shoes off later."

Kitty stared down at the expensive shoes on her feet, looked
at the stall, looked at Rein's broad, sheepskin-covered back, bit
her tongue, and got the bucket. The next day she borrowed
boots from Gabriel when she followed his lover into the barn.

"Put this bale up there," Rein said, pointing. Kitty jumped,
realizing that she had lost the thread of conversation while staring at Rein's hands. They were big for a woman's, callused, with
nails cut down to the quick. She dug her own nails into her jeans
pockets, feeling where the jeans were getting too tight. Her hips
were expanding with Gabriel's cooking. Then she realized what
the big woman was asking her to do. "I can't lift that," she said.
"It's too heavy."

"Sure you can," Rein said. "You're not a weakling, and you
don't have a bad back."

"I can't," she protested several times, and each time Rein
countered with the surety that she could, indeed, do it. It was an
unfair trap. If she didn't try, she was a weakling, and she very
much did not want to be a weakling in front of this Valkyrie. If
she *did* try....

She tried, and there was much struggling, and red-faced gasping, but the bale ended up on the shelf on top of the other ones.

"There," said Rein. "See, you could do it after all."

Kitty bit her lip. Mostly she felt awkward, not triumphant. She hated sweating, and struggling, and being flushed and...and *pushing*. It was so unfeminine. It was the sort of thing butches did, or men.

Rein grinned at her. "You have girl disease," she said. Kitty stared at her in horror until she explained. "You've been taught all your life not to use your full strength, so you don't know how much strength you have. You don't know where your body's limits are, because you've never reached them. You always pull your blows. That's girl disease." She eyed Kitty for a moment, and then jerked her head toward the woodshed. "Come on over here," she said. "I'm going to teach you something.."

They stacked narrow logs in the sawhorse, and then Rein got out the chainsaw. "You're going to learn how to use this," she said.

"What!" Kitty squeaked in horror, one part of her weirdly anticipating something out of a bad splatter film. "I—you can't be serious! Those things can cut your leg off!"

"Only if you handle them wrong. Here, hold it. Just hold it for a minute, while it's off," Rein ordered. She never coaxed, just ordered. Kitty found herself lifting it, feeling its considerable weight in her hands, the rubber grip rough against her palms. "Ninety-nine percent of accidents happen because people violate two simple rules. First, never raise the thing above your solar plexus. Second, if it sticks, which it will eventually, turn it off before you pull it out. Now repeat that back to me."

Kitty did, and then a pair of earphones was slapped on her head. Rein pulled the string a few times, and the saw engine caught. The world seemed to be completely filled with its terrible roaring, and her hands shook as she took the evil machine from Rein's hands. No, she wanted to scream, I don't want to have anything to do with this. But once again, Kitty was more scared of the Viking—or of her disapproval, she briefly realized, then pushed the fleeting thought away uncomfortably—than of a roaring chain saw.

And then Rein was standing behind her, pressed up against her with her strong, competent hands over Kitty's, and they were moving the saw together through the wood that resisted and then parted with excruciating, precise slowness. She could smell sawdust and sheepskin and sweat, and feel the softness of Rein's big belly and breasts against her back. Log after log fell away, and nobody was dying or getting carved up, and while it couldn't exactly be called easy, it wasn't all that difficult, either. By the time Rein stepped away and let her make the last few cuts herself, she was grinning.

"I teach all the women who come here how to use it," the Viking said as she showed Kitty how to put it away. "After this, facing bureaucracies or angry lovers becomes a whole lot easier. Go ahead, say it. 'I can handle a chain saw.'" Her keen gray eyes found Kitty's brown ones and held them like a vise grip.

"I can handle a chain saw," Kitty breathed, eyes dancing, and suddenly realized that she was wet right through her jeans.

Teach me. The words seemed to be constantly on the tip of Kitty's tongue over the next few weeks, although she never actually spoke them aloud. Rein seemed to know, psychically, when she was thinking them, and taught her...how to change the oil in a car, and then how to change the valve cover gaskets. How to shear a sheep, how to spin wool. The fleece flowed through Rein's fingers while Kitty struggled with her drop spindle. She was getting used to struggling. How to split wood, how to milk goats, how to clip and dip the umbilical cord on a newborn kid.

Somehow, every time she said it in her head, *teach me,* it was like saying *fuck me*, or at least it made her just as wet.

Her nails broke off. *That's OK, I can regrow them.* Her designer jeans got ripped. *I can buy more.* It wasn't as if she had any intention of doing any of these things again—when she moved back to the city, she thought wryly, she'd go back to paying a mechanic and buying her food at the grocery store. It was that she wanted Rein to teach her strength.

Kitty finally did break down and ask Rein to fuck her. It was a particularly hot day, and they were out in the back field harvesting potatoes, both wearing nothing but cutoffs, ankle-deep in the soft earth. Kitty watched Rein's big Nordic feet plowing the dark soil as she wielded her shovel, watched them for a long time before she dared to look up and see the woman's big breasts swaying against her belly like sacks of flour. She wanted to press herself against those feet, feel them knead her flesh like they kneaded the earth, and what she wanted to do to those breasts...

She didn't know what had come over her, and she was mortified. Rein stopped, brushed back the flaxen strands that had escaped her braids, and squinted at Kitty, sitting among the clods, spade forgotten. "You OK?" she inquired.

Kitty didn't know how to ask. Actually, there was only one way to ask. She fumbled with the zipper of her cutoffs, got them down and her legs spread, there in the dirt. "Please," she said, putting all her frustration and longing into the word.

The Viking looked at her for a long moment, sea-gray gaze like frozen fjords. "I'll think about it," she said. Kitty felt as if she had been struck. It wasn't said the way Kay would have said it— *I'll think about it*, snapped out flippantly, meaning, *I want to, but only on my own terms.* No, from Rein it meant *I'm considering whether or not you're worth the trouble of interrupting this job.*

"Dig," said Rein. Kitty retrieved her spade and her shorts, and dug.

• • •

"Do a tarot reading, at least," Kitty asked later on. She felt as if she had no pride left. The Kitty of a month ago wouldn't have recognized her. "Find out if it's OK. Please."

"I'll think about it," Rein said, not taking her eyes off the spinning wheel as it whirred around and around.

• • •

Rein took her one day, finally—grabbed her in the barn and bent her over the hay bales, one hand on the back of her neck. The other hand yanked down Kitty's jeans and panties and thrust into her from behind. Kitty humped the invading fingers for all she was worth, her fists clenching in the hay as she strained against the strong hand that held her down. She came twice as the Viking rammed into her, first with three fingers and then with four. She tried for five, but it wouldn't work, and Kitty found herself vaguely ashamed. Not too much, though, for the orgasms had been too sweet after days of waiting. Then the fingers withdrew, and she heard the sound of unzipping.

"Your turn," Rein said. She took off her clothes and flopped naked in the straw, belly bouncing, laced her hands casually behind her neck, revealing twin blond fountains of armpit hair. "Impress me."

Kitty's other lovers had all been glad to pleasure her; honored, even. The more she'd moaned and writhed, the more they'd puffed with pride and been willing to do her long past the time when they'd been too tired to get done themselves. It had suited Kitty. Rein made her work. *I'm not a weakling.* If she could heave a bale, she could certainly lick Rein's cunt until her neck and tongue ached. If she could handle a damn chain saw, she could certainly fuck her until her arm felt as if it was going to snap in two.

The Viking's cunt was as capacious as the rest of her, and it ate Kitty's hand well past the wrist until she wondered if it would suck all of her in. Echoes of stories she'd read, of strange faerie creatures with cunts full of teeth, resonated through her. Was it faeries, or maybe dryads? She had thought of Rein as a great tree. What sort of dryad would live in a big old oak, or maybe a hundred-year-old sugar maple, with golden foliage and a trunk so broad that your arms could never reach around it? Surely not a little slip of a creature, more like something mountain-shaped that you could sink your arm into.

Kitty's other hand found Rein's breast, like soft, yielding earth, and squeezed a nipple the size of her thumb. She liked them squeezed hard; she'd demonstrated by grabbing Kitty's tit—"like *this*"—hard enough to elicit a yelp. *Femme does not have to mean incompetent. I am going to make this woman come if it's the last thing I do.*

Afterward, Rein cuddled her in the darkening barn and stroked her all over. Her hair had come out of the braids and Kitty rubbed herself with the thick blond mass, let it cascade over her like raw silk. Rein's thigh was shoved up between her legs like the broad back of a horse. She couldn't come that way, from rubbing on it, but it kept her clit happy for a long time while they kissed. The big woman's kisses were measured, reticent; she was still gauging how much to dole out to her unexpected visitor. Kitty wondered how much she gave to Gabriel. "Do you fuck the men in your life like this?" she gasped as the Viking's fingers found their way into her cunt again.

The thick blond eyebrows rose. "Of course," she said, as if it were self-evident.

• • •

Kitty's friend Julie, house-sitting her apartment, called every week just on principle. "Kay comes by sometimes. She sits in front of the house and watches, just watches. Once I went out and knocked on the car window, told her that you didn't live here anymore."

"That probably wouldn't work," Kitty said, clutching the phone with a white-knuckled grip. "My suncatchers are all still in the window."

"Want me to take them down? I can."

"OK, I guess...." She forced herself to relax. "Look, she's not going to burn the place down or anything. Kay isn't that violent, she just lost it that one night. I simply don't want to face her." Because sorting out whose fault it really was would be so much of a headache that it's just not worth it. *Give it up, Kay. Give. It. Up.*

"So when are you coming back?"

"I don't know...eventually, I suppose." *When I've learned enough.*

• • •

Rein put Kitty's legs in the air and ate her, pressing her knees out so that she was spread wide, pulling her labia apart and using her tongue from clit to tailbone until Kitty screamed. Then she kicked her out of bed and let Gabriel in. The next morning she hand-fed Kitty pieces of French toast with maple syrup, explaining as she popped each piece into the girl's mouth how they tapped the sugar maples and boiled down the syrup. "Let me do you again tonight," Kitty begged between bites.

"We'll see," Rein said, silencing her with another sticky fingerful.

"I have to go into town tonight," Gabriel said helpfully, adjusting his Indian print skirt and grinning at no one in particular. He added, "As you well know, Reinhold, darling."

"Like I said, we'll see." She allowed a small smile for them both.

• • •

Rein was on her hands and knees on the bed, with Kitty fucking her from behind, one hand wrist-deep in her cunt and three fingers of the other buried in her broad, magnificent ass. The big woman's breasts and belly swayed with every thrust. Kitty had always hated men who stared at women's large breasts, but now she felt like a guilty voyeur whenever Rein was naked, unable to take her eyes off them, unable to stop stroking and squeezing and sucking on them. Thank God Rein wasn't one of those butches who couldn't stand having them touched. Kitty's cunt ached, too, in a different way, but that could wait. She was busy, doing something that she wanted to be good at. Working. Being good for something. When Rein came, growling and contracting around her bruised fingers, she nearly cried with relief.

"You'll have to go soon," the Viking said to her as they lay pressed together later. Kitty stiffened. "I'm not kicking you out," Rein said calmly, "but you have to go back and deal with things. Clean up your mess."

Kitty hid her face in Rein's chest. "Come with me. Help me do it. Please."

"No. I'm not going to be your daddy," Rein said patiently. "Or your mommy," she said a little sharply as Kitty buried her nose further into her cleavage.

"And you can't be my lover, not very often," Kitty whispered, "not unless I want to give up my life and live here."

Rein stroked her hair. "I'll be your guardian spirit," she said. "You can make offerings to me, every once in a while, and I'll watch over you from afar."

Kitty giggled in spite of herself. "How will I invoke you?"

"Try a telephone." Rein rolled onto her back and stretched. "In fact, every time you're sitting at home, feeling scared, call me and tell me what you wish we were doing together. Or if I'm busy or not home, write it down. Or think about it, even, and masturbate. If you're beating off, you aren't busy being scared." She took Kitty's wrists gently in her large callused hands. "Remember that you're stronger than you think, most of the time."

The last gift that Rein gave her was a carved walking stick, thick as her wrist and polished to a silky smoothness, still shaped in the contours of the tree it came from. "In case you might need it," she told her, and then kissed her lightly, still reserved. Kitty grabbed her and stuck her tongue down her throat, right there at the bus station. The Viking's eyebrows went up, but she didn't resist.

Kitty took a bus home. Letting herself into the apartment she hadn't seen in two months, she collapsed onto her bed. She found herself hornier than ever, but her fingers didn't seem to do the trick. She wished Rein had come back with her, missed the earthy scent of her body, her strength and softness like a mountain range under the sheets. Taking the stick, she rubbed the knob at its top against her cunt until she came. My guardian spirit.

For the next three days, whenever she got frightened that Kay would come over, she beat off. It never happened. On the fourth day, Julie told her the latest gossip: Kay had found a new girl. It was almost a letdown. "Why don't you go out to the club?" Julie asked. "You've always had luck there. You never come home alone."

"Nah, I don't want to bother. They all look alike down there."

"What?" Julie was shocked. "What do you mean?"

Kitty wasn't sure what she meant, but the next day while she stood on the porch getting her mail, she noticed a woman coming down the street. Although she clearly wasn't butch, or even dykey, something about her reminded Kitty of Rein. Actually, it wasn't mysterious at all. It was her heavy, round body, the way it moved under her ruffled cotton skirt, the way her feet found their way purposefully and firmly down the street. Kitty found herself staring at the woman's ample chest and forced herself to look at her face. The stranger pushed a strand of curly brown hair behind her ear and looked straight ahead, until a man on the street called out a name, a nasty name.

The woman stumbled as if it had been a missile aimed at her, and her firm stride faltered. Kitty's hands clenched on the knob of the stick and her jaw tightened. The man laughed, a snide laugh, seeing his target find its mark, and said something else, something unintelligible to Kitty's ears.

The stranger turned her head, and her dark eyes were hurt in a way Rein's never would have been. Rein would have thrown something back, something devastating, and not missed a step. This girl needed something more. *A guardian spirit.* Kitty raised the walking stick to her face, smelling it—the topmost inches were permanently stained now with her juices—and then lowered her hand and touched the stick quickly to her crotch. There was no rhyme or reason to it, it was just the right thing to do.

The man took a step forward and leaned on a pile of old pallets, derision in every line of his body. Just as he was opening his mouth to make another remark, the pile collapsed, going over with a crash that tipped him into the nearby stairwell, his remark lost in a string of curses. His voice cracked with embarrassment. Kitty pointed her stick at him and laughed, loud and hard. The girl looked up at her, gratitude in her eyes, even if she wasn't sure what she was grateful for, and then moved on.

Kitty watched her go, watched the sensuous fullness of her ass as she moved. It looked as if it was going to be a beautiful summer after all.

LIQUID PLEASURE

Gabriella West

The first few hours at the clothing-optional spa had passed normally enough. I'd soaked in the pools after my long drive north from San Francisco, had a strenuous massage from a tiny, bird-like woman who'd pressed all sorts of tender points I never knew I had, and reeled out of her office and back to the pools with what seemed like a ton of tension lifted off me. I felt light and graceful in the water, the warm afternoon sun shining down on my face, my creamy neck and shoulders, and the tops of my breasts.

Looking down, I wished I could touch my nipples. My whole body felt in need of a good stroking, of a more delicious release. But I was here alone, as always, and in the pool with me were the usual clusters of couples, looking deep into each other's eyes as they smiled and chatted in low voices. The warm pool was the social pool; it was OK to talk softly here. In the hot pool next door silence reigned, and beyond that the little cold plunge was usually empty, and even more serene. I could sit there as long as I liked and look at the trees, breathe the fresh country air, and meditate. But what I really wanted instead that evening, I was beginning to realize, was something more carnal.

I looked boldly at the women and men entering the pool. They all had what society would've deemed gorgeous bodies: tanned, brown, lithe. My own build was voluptuous and my skin pale, though the sun and the massage had brought a deep, healthy flush to my face. I had come here a handful of times and each time I'd gone away feeling restored and happy, but always with a tingle of dissatisfaction. I felt so sexual here, yet at the same time I might as well have been invisible, an overweight girl in my early twenties.

But then, I figured that my desires would most likely never be satisfied there anyhow. I wasn't looking for a boyfriend. The single men I noticed at the spa didn't tempt me, and I ignored them. Nor would I find a girlfriend there in that heterosexual scene. What obsessed me was a fantasy I'd had for a long time: a man and a woman inviting me into their bed for hours of caressing and penetration, fucking and sucking. I would probably think of it tonight, I mused as I soaked, as I lay in my sleeping bag in the dorm room, listening to a couple doing it next door, and that'd be the closest I would get to sexual satisfaction. I would lie there drifting off to sleep, deeply relaxed yet aroused, the rest of the room full of empty beds whose occupants were off getting lucky.

Under the water I gently stroked my nipple, imagining a woman's rosy mouth suckling and biting me, her fingers slipping into my pussy, her voice exclaiming at the wetness. I closed my eyes, leaning against the side of the pool, drifting.

She whispers in my ear that her boyfriend is going to give my pussy a long, hard pumping with his dick, but first she's going to show me how well she can eat me out. As she demonstrates, her lover kneels behind her, fondling her ass, spanking it. She moans into my cunt, her tongue flicking in and out the way I love it, and as her tongue probes me skillfully, his lubed cock slides into her. I try to watch, but my eyes are fluttering and my face is burning. I close my eyes, listening to the delicious lapping of her mouth on me mixed with the louder, raunchier sounds of his cock working inside her, flesh slapping against flesh.

They don't really have names or faces. These dream lovers are always anonymous, always eager, getting down to it right away with no nervous preliminaries.

Would I really have the courage to do it, I wondered, if the situation ever arose? Probably not.

The sun was setting, and the water felt slightly chilly as I began to think about what to do with my evening. The truth was that, despite my fevered imaginings, I had only slept with a few people: a couple of men, a handful of women. They'd mostly been one-night stands, enough to know how good physical intimacy could feel, but not enough to rid me of the feeling of being clumsy and awkward, ashamed of my body, a little frozen and shy. Shaking myself out of my lingering fantasies, I wondered a little sadly why anyone would want me.

A couple beside me was kissing. Making out in public was discouraged at the spa, but always seemed to happen. People politely averted their eyes, each in their own little bubble. It tantalized me that I was close enough to touch them, close enough to put my hand on her plump breast, just as he was doing now. She was the only woman in the pool with full breasts besides me, I noted. They were both large-boned and tall, and seemed utterly at ease with themselves. She had lovely, dark hair and he did too, dark and curly. That made it even less likely that they'd be interested, I thought, for my hair was dark too…and didn't opposites always attract?

As he cupped his hand on her breast and bent to kiss her nipple, she smiled at me. I blushed, giving a hesitant smile back.

"Sorry for staring," I said in a low voice. "You just look..."

"Blissed out?" she said with a laugh. "It's not as if he hasn't been at me for the last two hours. Jeez, I thought you'd at least give me a rest in the pool!"

She spoke affectionately, and her partner raised his head.

"Honey, I've just given you three orgasms."

"So give it a rest now, babe."

He looked at me, shrugging. His eyes were very clear, shining and happy. They both looked like an advertisement for something, I thought. Something I would want. Something wholesome, actually. Maybe young campers, out on a hike. No, one of those weekly camping trips that I had never gone on, with bonfires every night and couples having surreptitious sex in their tents.

"The truth is, she's a total slut," he said, grinning. I glanced around. Nobody was looking our way.

"You seem embarrassed," the girl said.

"No; well, it's just...you obviously want to be alone...." I kept waiting to be dismissed, but they seemed intrigued with me for some reason.

"Hey, we've just spent two days here wallowing in each other. I think it's time to come up for air." She shook her thick mop of dark hair and I watched her despite myself, drawn by her vibrancy.

"I'm Angela," she said. "And this is my boyfriend, David."

"I'm Lisa."

"Are you a student?"

"Yeah, I'm doing my master's at State."

"That's funny, so are we!" As we chatted, comparing notes on our different programs (he was in science, she in drama, I in writing), I wondered about their banter earlier. Had they wanted to test me? Our talk was so mundane now, it was easy to believe we were clothed and at a party somewhere, sipping our first glasses of wine and making small talk. The only thing that kept catching my eye was the way Angela rubbed up against David. He was holding her gently from behind. Her lovely, large-nippled breasts bobbed on the water. I kept swallowing and trying not to look.

"Would you have dinner with us tonight, Lisa?" Angela asked quickly, out of nowhere. I felt a sudden twinge of nervousness and looked down.

"We promise not to bore you," David said. "We have lots of stories." When I met their gaze, they were both smiling at me.

"Does that mean I won't get any attention?" I joked.

"We'll give you lots of attention, won't we, David?" Angela inquired of her boyfriend, both of them nodding.

OK, I thought to myself. Just dinner. I had always disliked eating alone at the spa anyhow. It was the only part of the trip that seemed lonely to me. Dinner would be fine, and it seemed so unlikely that these attractive creatures walking out of the pool in front of me would want more. I hung back self-consciously, then forced myself to climb the steps, wishing the distance to my towel were shorter. As I wrapped it about me, I noticed them looking at me, and smiling. They're being kind, I thought. Nothing will happen.

Did I even *want* it to? Wouldn't I feel too guilty and freaky anyway?

They weren't lying about paying me attention, though. What I discovered over dinner, as we ate the spa restaurant's vegetarian fare and demolished the bottle of wine they magically produced from their backpack, was the fact that I, a single woman, alone and planning to spend the night chastely in the dorm, seemed oddly fascinating to them.

"Hey, it's a Saturday night—that can't be much fun," Angela murmured.

"It's all the fun I've ever had." Emboldened by the wine, I blurted out: "I've never gotten laid up here."

"Never say never," David quipped. We all laughed, and I blushed hard.

"She blushes adorably, doesn't she, David?" Angela remarked. I didn't dare to meet his eyes.

"Shyness is so endearing. I've never been shy. David's the shy one; he always tells me I have a big mouth."

"Useful in bed," David said, yawning.

She grinned. "Before I met David, I hadn't a clue. About anything. I had no idea how good life could be. I didn't even know I liked women. He was the one who talked to me about my fantasies. I'd never discussed fantasies with a guy before. What was the point?"

I didn't say anything. So there it was, out on the table. What would come next?

"And all my boyfriends before him were so fucking possessive. With David, my inner flirt has definitely been released. Hasn't it, hon?"

"I like to see her flirt with women," David said ruefully, rubbing his chin. "The problem is that the women she goes for would rather I wasn't around. I can understand that. I'm good at getting out of the way."

"I told him the next time I'd include him. It's only fair."

I still didn't say anything, gulping my wine.

"You're his type—soft and sweet. He loves real women, with big tits. Don't you, David?"

"Ah, stop it, Angie. You're being obnoxious."

"But I've been a loudmouth from the first minute we met her. I think she kind of likes it. I think she wants someone to take charge, to run the show. Is that what you want, baby?"

She looked at me, smiling. There was such a difference between her brassy words and her pretty face and warm eyes. It might've bothered me before, but now her aggressiveness seemed exciting. He was gentle, and that was exciting too.

"Maybe," I said, blushing. "Look, I don't really know what I want. I'm pretty inexperienced."

I sounded so goofy, I thought. So naive.

They exchanged looks. "There's no pressure," Angela continued, "but we'd like you to come back to our room and we can take it from there. Would you be up for that?"

I hesitated, then nodded.

• • •

I was lying naked in their bed. The room was dark and warm, lit by a lone candle that Angela had set on the table near the door. She was resting on my breasts. What shocked me was the tenderness I felt as I stroked her hair. Earlier, I had gripped it as she moved expertly between my legs, her tongue strokes sharp and strong and rapid on my clit. She had told me she would not be happy until I screamed with pleasure, and I had privately thought how unlikely that was, for I had never uttered more than faint moans during sex before. Something she did with her tongue, though, made my cunt come alive. I sobbed and begged and finally spasmed hard as she moved her fingers in and out of me like a pro, like a seasoned dyke. I wanted more. She could sense it, as she moved sensuously off my slick body, making room for David. He kissed my mouth, my breasts, his hand sliding down between my legs. He began to tell me how beautiful I was, how they had watched me as I walked out of the pool after them. "We saw you were nervous and self-conscious, and you had no need to be, no need at all. You should be proud of these fantastic tits, this belly, these thighs. God, you're so soft. And wet. Baby, you're so wet."

He bent down and began to lick me. I relaxed totally as Angela tongued my earlobe, kissed me lingeringly, her hands on my nipples and on her lover's hair.

"He's good, isn't he?" she whispered hoarsely.

"Yes," I murmured, and then "yes, yes...."

When he moved up and into me it felt almost liquid, despite the weight of his body, which added to the pleasure. His cock seemed to dip inside me, my legs wrapping around him in an instinctive movement. It had none of the fumbling of my few previous encounters with men.

"He's going to fuck you for a long time, aren't you, David?" Angela crooned beside me. "He can go for an hour sometimes. Do you like it, Lisa? Tell him how you want it."

He was big. He filled me completely up to the hilt. I gasped with every thrust, my eyes filling with tears.

"You love it, don't you?" Angela said, stroking my hair. I looked into her eyes.

She was staring at me, her eyes deep and focused. "He's fucking your brains out and you love it. Look at her eyes, David, they're going back in her head. She likes it rough. Give it to her, David."

He was fucking me with deep strokes, my cunt holding him in, my cries and moans involuntary. I could hear myself groaning "Fuck me, baby, oh, fuck me harder," like the starlets in porn movies whom I'd always suspected of faking it. But this was real. He would pause for a moment, sweat pouring down his face, and then start again, the pleasure all the sweeter for that brief hiatus.

He pulled out. "Get on your hands and knees," he said in a low voice. Angela moved in front of me and I buried my head in her cunt. I was mesmerized by her musky scent and large clit, which I teased with my tongue.

"Suck. Really suck it," she urged, her voice high and ragged. He was moving inside me slowly and steadily, and my whole body was trembling.

"God, her ass is beautiful. Look at that big, milky-white ass. And look what you're doing to my girlfriend's cunt. Naughty girl."

He pulled out, spanked me, pushed in again. "That's right, eat her cunt," he urged, banging me harder now, then stopping, slowing down, pulling out as if to tease me, slapping me again.

"Please," I wailed. "Fuck me!"

I began to thrust back against his cock. The fuck had become wild. He grasped my breasts from behind, squeezing them, his back pressing deliciously on mine as his cock moved ever faster. I lost track of time.

My fingers worked inside Angela. I tried to concentrate, and to my surprise she came hard, gasping, arching her back and collapsing.

David's fingers stroked my clit. As I came, the whole room seemed to quiver and fade away. I could vaguely hear him groan. He pulled out, and we all lay together in a sweaty mass of limbs.

"So how was it?" Angela asked sleepily. Ages seemed to have passed, the candle had fluttered out. Some people walked by outside, laughing, and then there was silence again.

I kissed her in response. I could barely think. My body had never felt this present, this satisfied, this real. I did not know how to put into words the gratitude and amazement I was feeling.

"Could you tell it was our first three-way?" David murmured.

"We aim for sophistication, but it's mostly bravado," Angela said. "Basically we wanted to give you a good time."

"I've always feel clueless in bed before," I said giddily. "But now I feel like a slut. An incredibly satisfied slut."

I stretched, enjoying the feeling of their warm flesh against mine. I didn't feel fat, I thought—just one of them. I could not hate a body that had been loved so well. Maybe it wasn't that simple, but at this moment I could almost love my body.

"You should've heard yourself begging for it," Angela said affectionately.

"You're not so shy in bed, you little sex goddess, you."

"I just loved the way you both fucked me, that's all. The way you took turns."

They chuckled at my earnestness. "We're not done with you yet," David said.

"Stay the night with us. We don't want you to have to go back to the dorm."

They wrapped their arms around me. In the morning, I thought, we'll make love again, in the sunlight. I won't be ashamed of my body. I'll be proud. And then we'll all go out to the pool together and stand in the water and talk. And people will look at us and wonder.

Because we're beautiful.

BIG GIRLS, LITTLE GIRLS

Lori Selke

The first time I saw Daniel Rowan, I knew. I wanted to sit in his lap and call him Daddy. Dreams of ruffled panties danced through my head like sugarplum fairies. I wanted to lick his lollipop, get my lips sticky with his sweetness.

I don't know if he was made to be a father, but he was definitely a Daddy through and through. Salt-and-pepper moustache, with kindly blue eyes balanced by a very wicked smile, eyes that spoke of an indulgent nature, and the smile of a dirty mind. The perfect combination.

I met him on a night ripe for snuggling close, a long winter evening at a holiday buffet, candlelight warming the walls as the weather outside frosted the windows. When the hostess introduced us, he looked me right in the eye. Do you know how many people refuse to meet my eyes? I'm not sure why. OK, sometimes it's because they can't lift their gaze from my chest, which can admittedly be somewhat distracting—especially when I try. But other times, their eyes just slide off me as if I were made of ice. Do they think I'm ugly? That I take up too much space? Whatever the reason, it's not worth my time to figure out. I cross these folks off my mental guest list right away (except for the bashful ones, who blush so nicely as they stare at their own toes—for those, I make a tiny exception and pencil in a second chance).

"I'm Daniel," he said. "Daniel Rowan."

"Like the tree?" I said, and then, "Selena, like the moon." And I thought, please don't let him kiss my hand or I might propose. But he just smiled that crooked smile and said, "Pleased to meet you, Selena-like-the-moon."

Right then our hostess dragged him away toward someone he just had to meet, apologized for the interruption, and promised to bring him back when she was done, but the spell was broken. Daniel gave me an abashed look over his shoulder as he let himself be led away.

So there was nothing else for it. It was time to ask around. I started with my best friend, Lola. "Do you know anything about that guy?" I asked, and pointed him out from across the room. Discreetly, of course. "He says his name is Daniel. Do you know anything about him?"

"Yeah, he's been around. Why do you ask?" Lola looked from him back to me, and said, "Uh-oh."

"What?"

Lola clicked her tongue. "Crushed out already?"

"We've barely met, so it's not a crush. Just a scouting mission. So tell me what you know, OK?"

Lola's eyebrows scrunched up; not a good sign. "Out with it!" I demanded. "He's married, he's not interested in girls, he's a fugitive from the law—what? You're not fooling me, you know," I added as she stifled a giggle with the back of her hand. "I want the dirt. Don't hold out on me."

"It's not a big deal," she said. "And I might be wrong. But I think he likes little girls. Not, like, underage," she hastened to add. "Although I think he likes playing Daddy." I definitely felt a tingle between my legs at that. I might have even run my hand across my butt once, unconsciously.

"I mean, physically. I think he likes them petite." Lola said, bringing me back to earth with a thud. She shrugged and took a sip of her cocktail. "Sorry. Don't shoot the messenger?"

It was bad news. I can be a lot of things, but physically small is not ever going to be one of them. I'm nearly six feet tall, and plush. Ample. Zaftig. Curvy. Big. All my friends say, "You're not really fat," which really means, we still think you're cute. And I am. But I'm not a little girl.

And it's only at times like this when I even have a twinge of regret about it. Because I like that tossed-around-like-a-rag-doll feeling as much as anyone. Plus, I'm sturdier than the factory-issue model, so you can be rougher, if you like. I'm not delicate, I won't break. But it would probably take a pack of men to take me down proper. If what you like is to cover me like a big old blanket, it's just not going to work.

Lola said, "He's a real sweetie, otherwise. I just wanted you to know that you might not be his type, so don't get your hopes up too high."

"Helium tanks on hold," I agreed. Then I crossed my arms and stuck out my lower lip. "Fudge," I said. I may have even stamped my foot.

"Consolation prize," Lola declared, and popped a mini cream puff in my mouth. "I think you should definitely at least pursue the friends-and-acquaintances angle."

I licked cream off my lips as she leaned in to whisper conspiratorially. "I hear he's a great cook, too."

I put a hand to my ruffled décolletage. "Be still, my heart!" I said, "You must reintroduce me." I took her hand and pulled.

The two of us practically cornered him—not that he seemed to mind much. By the end of our conversation, Lola had managed to invite him to dinner at my place, all three of us. Brilliant. She winked at me as we went back for champagne. I could have kissed her, but she said, "Save that for Daniel," and laughed when I turned just a little bit pink.

To be honest, I love being crushed out on someone. It adds a zing to everything. Every time you turn a street corner or walk into a store, That Special Someone could be there, too. You could be getting coffee and bagels one nippy Sunday morning, and he could be in line just two people ahead. You'd wind up chatting, walking home together, kissing on the front stoop. It's like living inside a champagne flute all the time, all giddy and bubbly and sparkly-pink.

The heightened sense of romance is the good part, sweets for love's sugar-tooth. The bitch is the unrequited part. For me, it actually aches, just below my navel and tight in my chest. Probably a waste of energy too, all this mooning and daydreaming. There's no relief for it. It's like emotional engorgement—without the orgasmic payoff, you just have to wait for the blood and passion to fade away, and in the meantime, everything's too tender to touch.

So I tried not to think too much about it until the time came. Lola, my co-conspirator, canceled out on dinner at the last minute as planned, telling Daniel that she'd come down with a little something. But of course, we shouldn't reschedule, she'd have another chance to get together with us later.

It was the perfect setup. Dinner at my house, on my turf. Originally a friendly get-together, but now with a chance at a more intimate connection. No pressure, but plenty of opportunity.

I fudged on dinner. Takeout sushi by candlelight. I think he knew what I was up to when he saw the table set, because he gave me that smile, with a little teeth and the glimmer of candlelight in his eye. I took his coat and draped it over the back of the couch.

After dinner, we retired to the couch for a little conversation. Now came the hard part. He'd been a good sport up to this point, taking my little dinner switcheroo in stride.

But what if he was just being polite? What if I'd been misinterpreting that smile he gave me over the cucumber roll? What if his intentions were entirely honorable and nothing more?

I tried not to sit too close to him, even though every stitch of me wanted to dump myself right in his lap until I was spilling out all over. Maybe he didn't like that. Maybe he liked things contained and tidy. I felt suddenly shy and flustered, and I swear I was blushing.

But before I knew it, he'd taken my hand and kissed the tips of my fingers. "I hope I'm not being too forward," he said.

So I leaned forward and kissed him, ignoring the fluttering in my chest. "Not at all," I said, and hoped I sounded confident and sultry.

We necked a little, I rubbed my tits against his chest, and when we took a break for air, I leaned my head against his shoulder and breathed out my anxiety. "I thought you liked little girls," I said.

I could feel his cheek curve into a smile against my head. "I make exceptions," he replied. "Besides," and he started to stroke my hair, "I may like them little, but that doesn't necessarily mean small."

I think I may have actually gasped. I know I sat up and looked him right in the eye.

"I can be little," I said. I looked down at my cleavage, my hips, my plump thighs. "I may not look the part, but I can. In fact,

I'd like that very much," and I felt something loosen between my legs at my own words. But I still couldn't say the D-word, not yet. Not until he accepted.

Which he did by kissing me, softly but assertively. Then he took my chin in his hand. "Such a pretty girl could get into a lot of trouble, couldn't she? I bet you're a wild one. I bet you need a firm hand." I could tell he was trying hard not to laugh, to keep us both from falling into a heap of giggles right there on the couch. But then his face turned serious. "Are you looking for a Daddy, little girl?"

And then I couldn't answer; I buried my head in his shoulder and squeezed his shoulder. Then he did laugh, and put his arms around me.

Eventually, I ended up half in his lap, with one of his hands up my skirt. Not insistent, just friendly, making its acquaintance. Two fingers hooked under the band of my underwear, but more or less holding still as I rocked against them. His face in my cleavage, kissing lightly. My own head was thrown back, and I was smiling.

And then there was sort of an awkward pause. His head lifted from my chest; he looked a bit sheepish. "Usually," he said, "the thing to do at this point is carry you off gallantly to the bedroom, but, ah..." he trailed off as he put his arm around my hips and tugged ineffectually. I couldn't help laughing. I slid out of his lap and looked over my shoulder at him.

"This way," I said, and flounced to the bed.

It went just as it should go. He kept his hands up my skirt, whispered things in my ear like "You're such a good little girl, letting Daddy touch you there. Do you like making Daddy happy? Will you open your legs a little wider for me?"

"It's my first time, Daddy," I said.

"Of course it is," he replied, and I turned molten.

So naturally it didn't feel at all like the first time when he finally slid his cock into me, so slowly it was almost torture. I wanted to dig my toes into the mattress and climb my way up that prick. I had been wearing white panties, just in case, but after they were out of the way, it was all smoothness and openness and liquid warmth. But I didn't mind. There would be other first times with my new Daddy and his big, tender hands, his maddening cock that was all the way inside me now, like a wick for the flames that were burning in my cunt. Daniel leaned over to kiss me on the forehead, and I clutched him to me, moving my hips urgently, and he took the hint.

"It doesn't hurt, Daddy, it feels so good, don't stop."

"I would never hurt you, my baby girl."

"Your big girl," I corrected. "I'm all grown up now, aren't I, Daddy?"

"Are you ever," he said, and smiled; sweat broke out on his brow, and he closed his eyes.

Eventually we stopped talking altogether.

I was right. There were plenty of first times after that for Daniel and me. We didn't always play Daddy games, but they were my favorite.

Sometimes, I would suck his cock for the very first time. Sometimes I would cajole him into showing me just exactly what Mommies and Daddies did together in the bed at night. He would bribe me with popsicles and other treats. I gave Lola my undying gratitude for setting up our first date so smoothly, and she's vowed never to let me forget it—nor to let me pay off the debt; better to hold it over me forever, so that I know my place.

And boy, do I. Right in Daniel's—I mean Daddy's—lap.

ETCHED IN THE FLESH

Sacchi Green

The lonely wail of the train whistle echoed through the empty place inside me as we pulled into Brattleboro. I needed Kaitlin so badly I couldn't think straight. Long train rides always get me horny—the vibration, the swaying undulation—and that wasn't even the half of it. This trip, the first without her in years, had stirred up emotions I just couldn't handle alone.

But Kait wasn't there to meet me. Instead, it was Jenna standing beside the station wagon holding out the keys.

"Where the hell's Kaitlin?" I asked, and Jenna winced. Why did she have to be so damned jumpy around me? With anybody else, customers, suppliers, even Kait—and I knew she had a thing for Kait; who wouldn't?—Jenna was all common sense and competence.

I tried to tone down my irritation. "Everything all right?" Nothing I'd just been through was her fault.

Funerals are such damned, surreal blips in time. Trying to play the dutiful daughter I'd never been, moving ghostlike among people and places so familiar I'd had to block the pain with distance, sensing my grandmother's emanations of love and hate as intensely as when she'd been alive...I was so disoriented that only Kait's warm, abundant flesh could anchor me in my own.

So maybe horniness *was* at least half of it. I even found myself eyeing Jenna. Not bad, but too young, too raw, marginally pert. Pert bores me. In Kaitlin's generous mysteries I could lose myself. In Kaitlin's generous mysteries....

Dammit, where *was* Kait?

"Everything's fine," Jenna said in a rush. "The shop's been really busy, and then that sales rep for the card company was late for her appointment, so Kait couldn't get away in time."

Made sense, but I still brooded. Kait knows what train rides do to me. Did she think I'd jump her right on the platform? Would she have minded? She didn't mind that time I demonstrated how really roomy the handicapped restrooms on Amtrak are. That's the kind of thing it's a kick to have done once, without wanting a repeat performance. She'd had striped bruises on her lower back for a week from the safety handrail on the wall. Flaunted them, too, in a backless halter-top.

Kait in a backless top. Or out of one. I hurled my bags into the station wagon with unnecessary force, turned to grab the keys from Jenna, and changed my mind. "Go ahead. You drive."

She stared in amazement. I can't stand letting anybody else drive, except maybe Kaitlin. I won't even take a bus. A train is about as much as I can handle; at least I don't have to see who's in control.

"Are you OK, Andri?" Jenna asked when I was settled uneasily in the passenger seat.

"Fine. Just tired." And just wanting to give you a vote of

confidence, I thought, with the added attraction of being able to close my eyes and visualize Kaitlin. "She could have let you handle the card order on your own. You have a good sense of what will sell."

The extra bit of reinforcement made her pale, freckled face light up. I watched her through half-closed eyes, since riding blind turned out to be more than I could manage, not to mention the fact that half an hour of visualizing Kait would make me so wet I'd be lucky to be able to walk without getting sore. And not to mention the tension that seemed to radiate from the paper-wrapped packet in my jacket pocket. "For Andrea's Woman" was scrawled across it in my grandmother's slashing handwriting. She'd left little bundles all over with people's names on them, declaring them sealed with curses so that nobody else would open them.

"Andrea's Woman." But she'd known Kaitlin's name perfectly well. I was tempted to risk a curse I didn't quite believe in, to make sure Kait wasn't in for some unpleasant surprise. The one time they'd met, the old termagant had pronounced that, since I'd damned sure never find a man who'd put up with me, it was just as well I'd found a good woman. That had seemed close enough to approval. I forced myself to stop fingering the packet and allowed myself to think instead about touching Kait, just a little, just the curve of her cheek, maybe down to the base of her throat, maybe just down to where her breasts begin to well...maybe to....

I sprinted for the back door of the shop before the car had quite stopped. The bedlam inside was intense. Tourists seem to descend on Vermont earlier and earlier every fall; there'd been no way we could both be gone at this time of year. It wasn't even the weekend yet, and peak color was at least a week off, but you'd have thought it was Provincetown in August the way they were milling around. And buying, too—books, crafts, cards, toys; at this rate we should make it through the rest of the year OK. I would have been elated if there hadn't been so much else on my mind, and if I hadn't seen the exhaustion on Kaitlin's face, in spite of her smooth handling of customers.

I slid behind the counter. "Take a break, Love," I said into her ear as I pressed my crotch against her magnificent posterior. She moved ever so slightly backward into my heat without missing a beat of making change.

"You must be tired after the long trip," she said, her voice doing that number on me it always does.

"You know damned well how I am after the long trip," I murmured, and smiled blandly at the harried father trying to get his kids to settle on their purchases. I massaged the nape of Kait's neck under her thick, russet braid. The muscles were tight. "You have a headache. Go get rid of it before I get home."

"Where's Jenna?" Kait glanced around, but Jenna was already forging order out of the chaos at the other cash register. Ricky, our new part-time clerk, hadn't handled a foliage season before.

"I'm on it," I said. "You go get some rest. Plenty of rest." I edged around and nudged her away from the register with my hip. She copped a substantial feel as she departed, leaving my ass tingling.

"See, guys," I said to the two squabbling boys, camouflaging my private grin in professional affability, "this model rocket goes higher, this one goes farther. But what matters most is skill. You want separate bags?"

Their father looked at me with relief, then added one of Kait's CD's to the pile. "Does this ever take me back!" he said. "I used to see you two at folk festivals, way back when. You wrote most of the lyrics, right? Really dug 'em. And Kaitlin...what a voice! "

"She's still got it," I said with feeling, and his knowing grin answered mine as he shooed the kids onward.

There are worse ways for folks to make you feel old.

A tour bus spilled its load outside just then, and we went into overdrive. Kait tried to come back to help, but I scrawled a note and shoved it at her. When she read it, she laughed and almost challenged me, but changed her mind.

"If you don't get your sweet ass out of here, I'm going to fuck it right across the counter," I'd written. And meant it, too.

Kait was in the garden when I got home, gleaning a few of the hardier greens that made it through September. "I didn't expect you so soon," she said, her rich, lazy voice affecting me like a lingering touch.

"Jenna offered to stay and close up after the last few stragglers."

I put my arms around her from behind and snuggled my face into her neck. She was wearing one of my old dirty flannel shirts with nothing underneath, so that my scent blended with her heady aura of honey and fresh bread and earth and arousal. HomeKaitlinHome....

"Jenna is a treasure," she said, as though she didn't notice what my hands were doing under her shirt, but her nipples told me otherwise. After the first compulsive cradling of her abundant, heavy breasts, I had eased off, circling my palms so that I just brushed the tips, making them strain for my touch. Which they did. Which made my own breasts ache, along with pretty much every other part of my body that could get my attention.

She started to turn in my arms. "Wait," I muttered, thrusting my knee between her legs, rubbing my crotch against her round, round ass. "You go full frontal and you're going to get it right here in the dirt and cabbages."

"It was fine in August, in the herbs," she said, that musical cello throb beginning in her voice, "but it's a little chilly now." She turned toward me anyway, slipping a hand between my thighs, pressing it up against my ache so that I arched into her touch and forgot to hold her tight.

"Come on, Andri, get a grip. You can make it!" Then, having made nearly sure I couldn't, she slipped out of my arms and dashed toward the house, unbuttoning the flannel shirt as she ran.

Not that the bed wasn't a good idea. But I caught her at the top of the stairs, and she let me press her against the wall, hard, as though trying to merge my whole body into hers. She reached up to stroke my cropped hair, raising her breasts high against mine, and I bent my face into their full, warm comfort, needing comfort, needing something else even more with an urgency that rocked me.

Cream, honey, silk; there's no adequate metaphor for the sweetness, softness, of Kait's skin. No way to describe the sounds she makes when I touch her, primal moans vibrating through her flesh from deep within. I worked my open, hungry mouth over her bountiful curves, growing more ravenous the more I devoured. I could do this forever, if the throbbing pressure in my groin would let me. Or if Kait would let me.

Her moans grew rougher. She forced my mouth onto a swollen nipple, and pushed my hands from where they'd been kneading her rounded belly down into the unzipped waistband of her jeans. And lower still. "Dammit, Andri, bed! And get your clothes off!" She scrabbled at my belt, but I held off a little longer, sucking and licking at one breast and then the other, working my fingers delicately over the hot, wet clit that was as engorged as her nipples.

Then she bit me, hard, on the side of my neck, and squirmed away, and threw herself on the bed. Watching her wriggle out of her jeans was so engrossing, I had a hard time fumbling with my own clothes.

As my jacket hit the floor I remembered the mysterious packet, but the heat of my blood and heart overwhelmed the chill of my grandmother's shadow. Mind and senses had a more compelling focus in Kaitlin's abundant flesh. On some deep, unthinking level, I understand the impulse that made our for-bears carve full-bodied goddesses out of stone and ivory. Who's to say some of those sculptors weren't women?

She stretched sensuously, grinned, and stuck out her long, mobile tongue; and when she arched her hips upward I was on her, no frills, needing nothing between us this time but our own heat.

Sometimes, when it hasn't been too long, when we can focus, yoga-like, with contemplative intensity, we can meet mound to mound, breast to breast, in slow, exquisitely precise strokes. Not this time. I straddled her, rubbing my wetness across her tender belly, then shifted so that I rode her thigh, mine pressed hard into her crotch. She clutched at my back, then my ass; her breathing came hard and fast, in counterpoint to mine. We moved against each other, with each other, and the tension mounted until I was dizzy with it.

"Now, Love, now, dammit! " Kate gasped, as harshly as her honeyed voice could get, and tugged at my arm. I braced myself with the other and slid my fingers over her damp mound, between her slippery folds, then deep, deeper into the hot, sweet, demanding mystery of her cunt.

She arched and writhed, and I picked up her rhythm, held it, accelerated along with her wordless, pleading moans; and at last she spasmed around my hand, and a sound like a chord played on a feral cello tore from her throat.

Better, more profoundly needed, than to come myself. As if I had a choice. Kait would never leave me hanging. She didn't wait to catch her breath before she began to work her mouth and hands over my body, and all my self-control began to melt, as always, under her touch. But suddenly the ripples of anticipation transformed into a violent shivering that my lowered defenses had no power to resist. "Kait...." Unshed tears burned in my throat.

"It's all right, Love," she said, knowing unerringly that what I needed now wasn't what I needed ten seconds ago. "I've got you safe."

And she did. Her warm, sustaining flesh moved over mine, her unbound hair flowed around me, sheltered me, formed a private space for the weakness that only Kait was ever allowed to see.

"She's gone, Kait! That vicious, domineering old woman...gone! And I never told her that I loved her."

"She knew." Kait kissed me hard and deep. "She knew," she repeated, coming up for air and leaning back. "She told me how hard it was, teaching you self-discipline, or as much as you ever did learn. She said the devil in you was nearly a match for hers."

"She told you that? But you only met her once!"

"Once was enough. We had a lot in common. But she made me promise not to tell you some things while she was still alive."

That sounded like the convoluted working of my grandmother's mind. I was still hurt. "All she said to me was that if I didn't treat you right she'd lay a curse on me."

"Damned straight, too, and don't you forget it." Kait wriggled against me, and the impulse to treat her really, really right began to revive, but she rolled off. "It's getting chilly; where's that shirt? If you ever desert me overnight again, Andri, be sure to leave me some flannel you've sweated into. It's good company. Maybe I'll even ask Jenna for a copy of the tape she made of us."

"What tape?"

"Didn't you know she listens to us, sometimes, when we get too enthusiastic outdoors?"

She knew damned well I didn't know. "But...she can't...."

"Let it go. I've talked to her about it."

I noticed she didn't say she'd told Jenna to cut it out. "I can't exactly blame her for wanting to hear you," I said, "but...."

"It's not me she wants to hear. It's you. She showed me her diary: 'Andri howls like a regiment of bagpipes going into battle, pennants flying, the sound enough to tear through flesh and spirit.'"

"Why the hell are you telling me?" I wasn't prepared to deal with his at all. I'd vaguely noticed bagpipe tapes being played in the apartment Jenna rents in our renovated barn, but I'd figured she was going through a phase of getting in touch with her Hibernian roots. At the moment I didn't want to consider what else she might be getting in touch with.

"Because she's right. That's what you do to me: tear through flesh and spirit, open me up, and fill me." She leaned forward and pressed her mouth hard into the hollow of my throat, which meant that her opulent breasts pressed hard against my ribs, and the smoldering ache began to flare again. "And maybe to caution you not to be too hard on her, but not to be too nice, either." Then she pulled away, even though my arms were tightening around her, and stood up.

"So," she said in a lighter tone, veering away from a subject she might not want to deal with just now, either. "Are you going to sweat a little for me if you have to leave me again?"

The way she flaunted her luxuriant ass as she crossed the room was meant to distract me. It did an outstanding job. "Sure," I said, "if you'll let me take along some of your seasoned underpants."

"Deal." She bent provocatively to scoop up my jacket, and the packet fell out. "What's this? A present?"

"A bequest," I said, and told her about the protective curse, bracing myself for whatever lay ahead.

"I can just hear her saying that." Kait hefted the packet, flat, with a thickly cylindrical object attached. "Shall I open it now?"

I wanted to say no, touch me now, I need you now, but somehow I had to get through this first. "What the hell. Why not?"

Kait turned on the bedside lamp and sat beside me, holding on to me without touching. She forced the knotted string off the corners of the package and peeled away the tape from the edges. "It's a picture in an old frame." We stared at a brown-tinged photograph of two girls arm in arm in front of an olive tree. My grandmother's dark eyes bored into ours from a face absurdly young to hold such challenge.

"Andri," Kait whispered, "that's just how you looked when I first saw you."

"No way," I said, but it was true, in spite of her antique clothes and long hair and the fact that I'm considerably taller. "Who is that with her?" It was a rhetorical question; I was startled when Kait knew.

"Her name was Allesandra. She was killed spying on the Germans in Sicily in 1943." Just from the way the girl stood, the look in her eyes, the way she filled out the peasant blouse and skirt, it was all too obvious how she'd been able to get close enough to spy. "Your grandmother showed me this picture and then...then she said, 'But I had my vengeance for her death!'"

"She *what?* How do you know all this? Why would she tell you and not me?"

"I think she just had to tell somebody, after all those years. Somebody who wasn't quite family."

Somebody who was Kaitlin. I couldn't resist pouring myself into her, and Jenna spilled the most intimate secrets, so why should I be surprised at my grandmother's vulnerability? But I had never been allowed to think of the arrogant old woman as vulnerable. Or even human.

"What else did she tell you? Did she say...were they...."

Kaitlin just nodded. Lovers. I looked down into the picture again. My grandmother's eyes, with a glint of fierceness even in that long-ago sunlit afternoon, told me what she had never told me in life. Dammit, she had owed me that much! I came close to hating her for what she had withheld, for what she had let me suffer alone.

And then I realized some fraction of what she had suffered.

"Vengeance? How? She must have told you more!"

"No. And I couldn't ask. It hurt her enough to go as far as she did. After that she changed the subject to gardening and gave me the seeds for that weird ridged zucchini I've planted ever since. The one you call 'the French tickler of the vegetable world.'"

The wild thought crossed my mind that the implacable matriarch of my family had, in fact, meant the seeds as just such a joke. Impossible. But.... I eyed the seven-inch brown-papered cylinder Kait was beginning to unwrap. No. Please, no. There are some things you just don't want to inherit from your grandmother, no matter what.

Kate glanced sidelong at me, and the corner of her mouth twitched. She knew perfectly well what I was thinking. "Don't worry. I think I can tell what it is." She went on unwinding coil after coil of paper, until the object's shape began to emerge, and when at last she held out the little stiletto-slim dagger I took it with something as close to reverence as I'm ever likely to feel.

"Her vengeance." I ran a finger along the blade. "It's cold," I said, somehow surprised.

Kaitlin stood and took the dagger from me, laid it flat in the deep valley between her breasts, and pulled me up so tightly against her that our bodies held the steel. "Her heart," she said. "Still fiery."

She was right. I felt its heat radiating outward, not from the blade alone but from fiery hearts back through the years. We pressed against each other, Kait clutching at my back, my hands filled with the glorious curves of her ass, rocking almost imperceptibly together.

Tension mounted as the need grew for flesh to move against beloved flesh. A fine and poignant torture, worth prolonging, except that the fear of the sharp edge shifting and slicing into Kait's delectable skin made me cut it short. And made me realize just how weak I really was.

I've always needed to feel strong—to split the firewood, shovel the snow, even carry Kait, in spite of her protests, across the occasional stream. Now, as I tightened the grip of my left hand on the compelling fullness of her ass and reached between the equally compelling swells of her breasts with my right, I faced my own deepest fear.

"I couldn't do it," I said, and tossed the dagger onto the bed. "I couldn't do what she did."

"Take vengeance?" Kate's green eyes looked deeply into my dark ones, knowing me so well that she already half-understood what I meant. "Nothing could have stopped you! I can see you now, going into battle with pipes skirling and banners flying, or slipping silently through the darkness if stealth was what it took."

I dropped my head to her shoulder and wrapped her even closer in my arms, thighs, everything that could grip her, trying to hold all of her inside me. "But you wouldn't be there to see me," I muttered into her neck. "I would avenge you, no question, preferably with tooth and claw instead of a knife. But afterward.... How did she go on living? I couldn't do that—go on without you."

Kaitlin had been stroking the nape of my neck, but at that her fingers tightened and her thumbs pressed into my windpipe just enough to get my attention. I raised my head.

"Don't!" she said fiercely. "Grieve for her, but don't judge her!"

"I'm not...."

"Yes, you are. You think she *shouldn't* have gone on, shouldn't have married, raised a family, given me you!"

"No!" There might be some truth to it. But it didn't matter. The thought of life without Kait was what tore me apart.

"And don't even think about losing me, because you never will!" Her green eyes were brilliant with anger, or unshed tears, or both. She dropped her hands to my shoulders and then, in strokes so hard and furious they hurt, ran them over all of my body she could reach while I still held her so tightly. "And if...if you ever dare to say that this flesh I love wouldn't go on, if only to carry the memory of mine, I'll take that knife, Nazi germs and all, and carve my name into you where you won't ever forget it!"

My grip on her had loosened a little, maybe to give her hands more territory to punish. She managed to get them on my breasts, and then, while I was distracted, twisted away from me and picked up the knife. She backed off a step and raised her arm—and even then, even as the blade shot past me to lodge, quivering, in the wooden headboard, the undulation of her flesh in motion sent resonating waves through mine.

Then she pushed me down onto the bed, and followed to nuzzle all along my inner thigh, making me melt and tense in ecstatic contradiction. "So," she murmured between kisses turning into bites, "just where shall I mark you? Here...or here where your fine Sicilian fur would hide it...or in this tender hollow...?" She teased me, stroking and licking until my readiness verged on pain and I arched into her touch and fought to control the raw cries clawing at my throat—a battle I needed more to lose than win.

"Kait!" My voice was knife-edged with desperation. The teasing ceased, as her wide mouth moved wet and hot and demanding against my pounding clit. Tongue, hands, divinely heavy breasts pressing my thighs; no need to sort it out, no need, impossible, to keep control. She drove me surely on and on, making my voice tear free from all restraint, forcing the agonizing tension to swell, and surge, and burst at last into dark, searing brilliance.

As peace flooded in behind the slowly ebbing glow, I pulled Kait up along my body until I could kiss her, deeply, and feel her tongue on mine. I'm never more sure of who I am than when I taste myself on Kaitlin's mouth.

We lay entwined, her thigh pressed gently now against my still-throbbing mound. I began to move my mouth over her seductive skin again, and felt her ripple of response, but I felt something else, too, something I recognized. I wasn't surprised when she swung her wide, powerful hips to the edge of the bed and stood up.

She crossed to the open window, and for an instant I wished I were watching from below, seeing Kait's curves outlined in the lamplight, and wondered whether Jenna might be out there. Then I went to stand beside her, looking out over the valley at the mountains dark against a twilight sky of Maxfield Parrish blue.

Kait gripped my hand and held it against her breast. I felt, more than heard, the tremor deep within of music being born. A fragment of melody took shape, evoking the mountains before us; then came a subtle change of tone, in that mysterious way Kait has of overlaying the mellow richness of her voice with a harsher power. The tree-furred slopes became the stony sides of Sicily's bare mountains, far away in space and time.

The tune faded, but the music was still in Kait's low voice when she spoke. "Write the words for me, Andri. Her story. Her song."

"Yes," I said. "'The Sicilian Dagger.'" Images, phrases, already stirred in my subconscious. "It's coming." My throat was still raw from cries I had made without hearing, drowned out by the storm within. I put my arms around her and bent my face into the soft, sweet warmth of her shoulder. "But for now, just hold me."

She knew how deeply into me she was already etched, with no need of any blade. She knew, too, when it was time to set thought aside and let the flesh tell what was in the heart; and, when comfort gave way again to hunger, she let me tell her once more all that burned in mine.

FRANK MILLER, 1984

Susan L. House

Frank Miller, crossing Wabash Avenue on his way to work,
is a tired old fat man, walking slowly as though his back hurts
and maybe his feet, too.

Frank Miller, on stage, settles into his chair. He pulls his cello
between his thighs, easing its big curves against him,
and strokes its strings. He makes it sing.

Frank Miller, walking to work, is a fat old man. Tired. World-weary.
Frank Miller, on stage, is a powerful man: strong and gentle,
        making love to his cello. Making music.

From my balcony seat, I can see that my big curves would fit
        between his thighs.

"I will rest against you and you will stroke my belly and make
     me sing,"
I whisper from high above.

I vibrate with the frequency of each note as he draws his bow
     across
his cello, across my belly, as I close my eyes and just listen.
I vibrate with the frequency of each note as his long fingers
     dance along
the cello's neck, massage my neck, as I close my eyes and just
     listen.

Frank Miller, make me sing.

ABOUT THE AUTHORS

Helen Bradley is an Australian-born cybergrrl, journalist, and writer who met the butch of her dreams in a lesbian chat room. She currently lives and writes in California. Her nonfiction is published internationally, and her erotic stories have appeared in *The Lesbian Erotic Cookbook, Cosmopolitan* magazine, *Hot and Bothered 2,* and *Best Lesbian Erotica 2000*. Her writing displays her profound love of big butch women, and she acknowledges a particular debt of gratitude to two—"the bee" and jd, who have each, in their own special way, nurtured and inspired her stories—and to her cat, Peaches, who reminds her of the importance of taking time out to enjoy a place in the sun.

Eleanor Brown is a freelance writer and graduate student of English literature. Born and raised outside Washington, D.C., she lives in Philadelphia. She writes erotica and other stories of love, sex, power, and infidelity. Her work has previously appeared in *CleanSheets* (cleansheets.com).

Heather Corinna is the founder and Editrix-in-Chief of *Scarlet Letters* (scarletletters.com) and *Scarleteen* (scarleteen.com). Her work has appeared online at *Maxi, LeisureSuit.Net, Orato, CleanSheets,* and *Other Rooms,* among others, and in the anthologies *Viscera, The Adventures of Food,* and *Aqua Erotica.* Her work in positive-sexuality activism and education has received many accolades, from *The Industry Standard* to the Illinois Library Association, *The City Pages* to *Playboy;* and even the Kinsey Institute finally picked up on the fact that she's been up to much good. She lives in the Minneapolis, Minnesota, with an extensive zoo and a stunning androgyne, and has achieved the medical miracle of living for thirty years on nothing but coffee, cigarettes, and stubbornness.

Dawn Dougherty is a juicy babe who lives outside of Boston. Her work has appeared in such illustrious places as *Best Lesbian Erotica 1999* and *2000,* and *Scarlet Letters* (scarletletters.com), In addition to her writing career, she is part of the high femme erotic drag trio The Princesses of Porn.

Sacchi Green leads multiple lives in western Massachusetts and the mountains of New Hampshire. She's published a modest number of science fiction and fantasy stories, but the erotic side of the force seduces her all too often. Some of the results can be read in the 1999 and 2000 editions of *Best Lesbian Erotica* as well as in the upcoming anthologies *Set in Stone* and *Best Women's Erotica 2001.*

Susan L. House lives, loves, writes, and lusts after cellists in Chicago.

Debra Hyde is a busy emerging author. She tracks sex and sexuality in the news on her weblog, *Pursed Lips,* and writes a BDSM column, "Leather and Hyde," for About.com. Her erotic fiction has appeared in several publications, including *CleanSheets* and the *Mammoth Book of Historical Erotica.* You can find her newest fiction in the e-chapbook *Y2Kinky* and in the soon-to-be-released *Desires* anthology from AmarMira Press.

Veronica Kelly has been published in the *Mammoth Book of Historical Erotica* and the e-book *Y2Kinky—Erotica for the New Millennium* (www.dreams-unlimited.com) as well as in the forthcoming erotic political anthology *Strange Bedfellows.* She is an upstanding citizen in a midwestern town. She votes in all elections and spies on the comings and goings of the neighborhood. She readily calls the cops on loud neighbors and gladly invites to her house for cocktails anyone who has a nice collection of jazz CDs. Ms. Kelly works in the communications industry and community theater. She is married and has one child.

Jianda Johnson lives in Southern California. A freelance writer, she is also a singer, musician, and filmmaker. On and offline, her fiction, nonfiction, and poetry have been published in *CleanSheets* (cleansheets.com), *Doorknobs and Bodypaint,* About.com, *Libida* (libida.com), *Scarlet Letters* (scarletletters.com), ChickClick.com, in University of California–Irvine's *Faultline* and *Womyns Quarterly,* and in Alyson Publications' *Faster Pussycats* anthology.

Diana Lee is a 46-year-old lesbian living in New York City with her cats, Tiger and Hanachan, who rule her life with iron paws. She has degrees in psychology and philosophy, and she has spent five years living in Japan, studying pottery. Among her passions are making leather toys and fetish wear, and writing about women loving women. Her first novel, *The Sign of the Wolf*, was published in 1998 in Germany. Currently, she is working on her fourth novel, *Blood Price*, a vampire mystery set in New York.

Catherine Lundoff lives in Minneapolis with her beloved partner and cats. She temps, writes, and is a member of an anarchist bookstore collective. Her writings have appeared in *Such a Pretty Face: Tales of Power and Abundance, CleanSheets* (cleansheets.com), *Lip Service,* and sundry other erotica and science fiction anthologies. She can be found at various alternative art spaces and the occasional science fiction convention.

Melusine lives and writes in Boston and has been published in *Consent, Black Sheets*, Necromantic.com, and *Blood Moon Zine*. She has worked as a graduate student, English teacher, and phone sex operator. She delights in black eyeliner, corsets, and wicked friends. Melusine also gives special thanks to her Master and her partner, who have provided much support and inspiration, as well as thanks to her professors in Restoration and eighteenth-century literature who now know what she was really thinking.

Corbie Petulengro is a pansexual writer who actually does cook on a woodstove, milk goats, and do needlepoint. She is a professional costumer, who loves any excuse to dress someone up.

Lori Selke lives in San Francisco and works intermittently. Her stories can be seen in places like *Black Sheets, Alice Magazine, Scarlet Letters, Best Bisexual Erotica, Leatherwomen 3*, and other groovy joints. She doesn't drink coffee or alcohol (much) and quit cigarettes years ago in favor of more esoteric vices.

Anne Tourney has published erotic fiction in various journals and anthologies, including *Paramour Magazine, CleanSheets, Best American Erotica 1994* and *1999, The Unmade Bed,* and *Embraces: Darker Erotica*. She lives in the San Francisco Bay Area with her husband and their pet sausage.

Reyna D. Tutto originated in an immigrant family mired in the Midwest. She escaped the flatlands, and currently earns a living by teaching other people's children. Convinced that the sense of smell is the sense that goes most directly to the erotic parts of our brains, she dabbles in formulating erotically stimulating perfumes. She plans one day to become obscenely wealthy, just as soon as she perfects the formula for a scent that instantaneously induces a sense of postorgasmic bliss.

Gabriella West earned a master's degree in creative writing from San Francisco State University. Her work has appeared in the anthologies *Early Embraces* and *Hot Ticket: Tales of Lesbians, Sex and Travel*. Other recent credits include the 'zine *Zaftig!* and *The Literary Review*. Her first novel, a lesbian historical romance, will be published by Dublin-based Wolfhound Press in 2001. She grew up in Ireland, which makes writing erotica even more fun. Thanks to Shar Rednour and Jackie Strano for unknowingly providing the inspiration for "Liquid Pleasure."

ABOUT
THE EDITOR

Hanne Blank's work as a writer, editor, and educator includes *Big Big Love: A Sourcebook on Sex for People of Size and Those Who Love Them* (Greenery Press, 2000), the groundbreaking book on body size and sexuality described by one reviewer as "...the perfect balance between expertise and humor...American sex-book-ese at its best," and *Best Transgender Erotica* (Circlet Press, 2001). Co-editor of the award-winning sexuality websites Scarletletters.com and Scarleteen.com, she is also a columnist, essayist, and fiction writer whose work has been featured in venues ranging from Susie Bright's *Best American Erotica*, the *Boston Phoenix, BBW Magazine, Lilith,* and *Bitch: Feminist Response to Pop Culture* to *The Elvis Presley Reader*. Hanne Blank lives in Boston with many houseplants, two cats, and one life partner. She can be found online at www.hanne.net.

"Denial" is dedicated her her friends Jim DeRogatis and Lou Kipilman, hunky fat guys extraordinaire.